# DANNY ORLIS
## AND THE
# ALASKAN HIGHWAY
## ADVENTURE

# DANNY ORLIS

## AND THE

# ALASKAN HIGHWAY ADVENTURE

BERNARD PALMER

*Danny Orlis and the Alaskan Highway Adventure*
© 2024 by Bernard Palmer
All rights reserved. First edition 1972.
Second edition 2024.



*Cover image: Adobe Firefly*

*Character illustrations: John Ball*

*Editor: Charlene Miskimen*

Aneko Press Youth

www.anekopress.com

Aneko Press, Life Sentence Publishing, and our logos are trademarks of Life Sentence Publishing, Inc.
203 E. Birch Street
P.O. Box 652
Abbotsford, WI 54405

JUVENILE FICTION / Religious / Christian / Action & Adventure

Paperback ISBN: 979-8-88936-072-8

eBook ISBN: 979-8-88936-073-5

10  9  8  7  6  5  4  3  2  1

Available where books are sold

# CONTENTS

# CHAPTER 1

# OPPORTUNITY FOR ADVENTURE

Sandy Cole and her mother, Gladys Fenwick, had reached a deadlock in their discussion. Now they stood glaring at each other as the silent seconds went by.

"But, Mother!" Sandy exclaimed. It was exasperating when her mother was so unreasonable. "*All* the kids are going."

"That's *not* quite true," Gladys Fenwick retorted. "I've talked with half a dozen of my friends. Their daughters haven't even *heard* of this trip to Alaska."

"But that's not what I meant," Sandy protested. "All the kids from *church* are going."

Gladys humphed. "I might have known it had something to do with that dear church of yours."

Sandy cleared her throat uneasily. She had known it was going to be hard to talk to her mother about going to Alaska with the church youth group. Mrs.

Fenwick never had been interested in her doing such things, and it was even worse now that her former husband, Brad Cole, had confessed his sin and turned his life over to Jesus Christ. As far as she was concerned, the church was a bond between her daughter and Brad. Even though she had remarried a few months before, she still resented every moment her former husband spent with their daughter, and she was determined to keep them apart.

"And just what is the purpose of this trip?"

"It all started when Mr. Robinson spoke at church about the need for short-term workers in Alaska." Sandy became vibrant as she launched into the story. "Someone made the remark that we ought to try to help them; and the first thing we knew the kids were so excited about it, they began to make plans. Some of the adults got interested, and it wasn't long until everything was arranged."

"I see." Her mother sniffed. "It's the most ridiculous thing I ever heard of! I can't understand responsible adults letting kids go off on such a trip!"

Sandy fought against the tears that rushed to her eyes.

"I suppose that father of yours approves. After all, it's for that *beloved* church!"

"I wasn't going to tell you this, Mom." The words caught in Sandy's throat, and she stared across the room miserably. "But I can't keep it from you. Dad's going along!"

There! It was out! Now Mom probably wouldn't let her go at all.

Mrs. Fenwick's eyes widened in anger. "So *that's* the reason you're so anxious to go running off to the end of the world." Her bitterness spilled out. "It'll give you a chance to spend three months with your precious father. I suppose *he's* the one who talked you into going!"

Mrs. Fenwick's fingers trembled as she pulled her robe tighter about her neck. She didn't know why Brad didn't get out of her life and leave her and Sandy alone. Hadn't he already caused them enough trouble?

He could talk all he wanted to about being a Christian and having a new life, but she knew better. He hadn't changed. Not him! This was only part of the act to make Sandy think he was different.

"Don't try to tell me that, Sandy," she said icily. "It was your father's idea not to tell me he was going along, wasn't it?"

Sandy was indignant. "He would've been furious with me if he found out I even *thought* of not telling you."

"Now, my dear, don't try to tell me anything about Brad Cole and what he wouldn't do. I know him much better than you do."

Sandy's lips trembled, and she was close to tears. Why did every conversation about her dad turn out this way? Her mother wouldn't give him credit for *anything.*

"Even if you hadn't told me, I would have found out."

"I know that," Sandy said desperately. Why should she even try to explain? Her mother wasn't listening. "I was tempted to try to keep it from you until after we were gone, but I didn't because I didn't want to deceive you."

Her mother's expression softened, and a weak smile appeared briefly on the taut line of her mouth. "Come over here and sit down, Sandy. There's something I want to tell you."

Slowly, she crossed the room and sat on the edge of her mother's bed, her young figure stiffening against the persuasion that was about to come.

Sandy loved her mom. That was what made all of this so difficult. She loved both of her parents.

"I know this is hard for you," Mrs. Fenwick said, "but I have some news that might make it a little easier for you to make up your mind. Robert and I have been planning a delightful trip for the three of us this summer."

Sandy's fingers were intertwined, and she tightened them nervously. She might have known her mother would try to bribe her. It used to be that Mrs. Fenwick tried to bargain with her daughter by promising Sandy some new clothes or redecorating her room. Now it was a trip.

"You don't even seem interested."

"I'm sorry, Mom, but I really and truly want to go to Alaska with the kids."

"You mean you'd rather go there than to Los Angeles?" her mother asked in disbelief. She didn't see how anyone, given such a choice, could decide against the glamorous West Coast city.

Sandy did not answer. There was no use arguing with her mother once her mind was made up.

"Robert is going to southern California to do some work for his company this summer," she went on. "You and I would have a whole month or more to go shopping and visit Disneyland and see the homes of the movie stars. We'll do anything you want to for the whole time. How does that sound?"

"You know what I really want to do," Sandy told her, "but I'll do whatever you say."

"You don't sound very happy about it."

Sandy choked back her anger. And why should she? She would rather stay home than be dragged halfway across the country to spend the whole summer with her mother and Robert. While the rest of the kids would be doing exciting things at the Northern mission station, she would be going to the places *they* wanted to see.

There was no chance for her to go to the forty-ninth state with the kids now. That was evident in her mother's voice. There would be hours of talk on the part of her mother, trying to convince her to make Los Angeles her own first choice for the summer; but in the end, the decision would be made for her.

Sandy dreaded having to tell the group, especially her best friend, DeeDee Davis.

DeeDee and her triplet brothers, Del and Doug, made their home with Danny and Kay Orlis, since their missionary parents were drowned in Guatemala several years before. She would have no trouble getting permission to go; neither would most of the other kids. Every day someone else exuberantly announced that he had permission to go.

In the week that followed, the trip to Alaska was the chief topic of conversation when any of the girls and guys were together. There were endless discussions about what they should take along and the things they would do on the trip. Sandy stayed away from them as much as possible; and if she couldn't avoid being with them, she remained silent and hoped nobody would ask about her own plans.

She might have known DeeDee would want to know whether she was going to make the trip; they were together most of the time.

DeeDee was greatly disturbed when she learned that Sandy's mother was opposed to the trip. "I thought it would be easy for you to get to go. After all, your dad's going along."

"That's the big hangup."

"Oh." She understood. They were such close friends they didn't have any secrets from each other.

Before they parted that night, they agreed to make

Sandy's getting to go to Alaska a matter of prayer between them.

"But I don't think it will do any good," Sandy said wearily. "I know my mother. She wouldn't care where I was going or who I'd be with. She wouldn't want me to be there if Dad was going to be there too."

As the days passed, excitement about the trip to Alaska increased steadily. Money was going to be a problem for some, but the kids were furiously working at odd jobs and saving most of what they earned.

The youth group held a Saturday car wash that was highly successful; and they set up a clearinghouse for anyone in Fairview who wanted to have his lawn mowed or raked and the gutters cleaned out or any other small jobs taken care of. It was surprising to everyone who was involved with the project how rapidly the funds came in. The last obstacle to the trip North was overcome.

"There's only one thing wrong, Danny," Del Davis complained the night the announcement about the money was made. "You and Kay won't be going with us."

"I sure wish we could."

Kay, too, tried to keep from showing her disappointment. It would be good to spend time with the kids from church on a trip such as this. She longed to be a part of it.

Danny helped with the project as much as he could in spite of the fact that he and Kay weren't able to go. He helped overhaul the church bus, checking the engine, and putting new tires all around. Knowing how hard the Alaskan highway could be on casings, he insisted that they buy two extra wheels and tires. When he and one of the other men in the church finished with the bus, he had the best mechanic in Fairview go over it, pronouncing it in excellent condition.

"I wouldn't be afraid to start for Alaska with this vehicle. It's in tip-top shape," the mechanic informed him.

The final week before the kids were to leave, Sandy's mother still had not relented. She talked fervently about the fun they would have in California, as though her own excitement would somehow be instilled in her daughter. Sandy tried to act interested, but that was difficult when all she could think about was the good time she would miss.

She had gone to bed that night and was almost asleep when the voices of her mother and Robert Fenwick drifted in from the living room. She wasn't trying to listen to what they said, but she couldn't avoid hearing it.

"I couldn't help noticing the way Sandy looked at you when you were talking about our trip to LA, Gladys. I don't think she really wants to go."

"That's Brad's doing. He's filled her so full of talk about the trip to Alaska that she can't think of anything else."

"I don't know whether Brad's responsible or not," he said. "The guys downtown say that half the kids in school are talking about going North with the bunch from that church. John Bailey said they could fill six buses if they took all the kids who'd like to go."

Gladys Fenwick's voice rose angrily. "I didn't expect *you* to stick up for Brad."

Sandy heard Robert's recliner sliding upright and then his pacing noisily across the floor.

"I'm not sticking up for anybody. I'm simply trying to tell you that you could be wrong about the reason Sandy wants to go wherever it is her friends are going. It just makes sense to me that she'd want to be with the other kids, regardless of whether Brad is going to be along or not."

"But you don't know him. He'll do *anything* to drive a wedge between Sandy and me."

Sandy recognized the tone. In a moment her mother would be crying, and the discussion would be over.

If Sandy's mother did start crying, however, Robert chose to ignore the tears. "This is really none of my business," he continued, "and I've tried to stay out of it; but for the life of me, I can't see why you're so opposed to it. She'll be well supervised, and I know she'll enjoy herself a lot more than she would being stuck with the two of us for the whole summer."

"You don't know her very well," Gladys went on petulantly. "She enjoys being with me."

"Sure, she likes to be with you, but at her age she'd a lot rather be with DeeDee and Brenda and the rest of their group. If you don't believe me, start talking with her about that trip and watch her eyes."

"You make me feel like a witch." Gladys Fenwick's voice trembled. "But I know what's behind all of this. It's Brad, and he's doing it because he wants to cause trouble."

Robert ignored her protest. "There's something else I have been thinking about. It would be nice for us to have the summer alone. Going out to LA together would be almost like a honeymoon."

Sandy was listening intently now, but her mother's voice was so small, Sandy couldn't hear what she said.

At first, hope sprang up unbidden that she might be able to make the trip. Of all the people she could have expected to stand up for her, her stepfather was the last. He was the only one her mother couldn't accuse of being on her father's side. Maybe she would get to go after all.

But that would be too much to hope for, she realized. Her mother was married to Robert now, but she still hated her dad and everything he tried to do. With him going along, Sandy knew that she didn't have a chance. It was all she could do to keep from crying again as she began to pray silently.

The following afternoon, Sandy was surprised by her mother's sudden announcement. "Robert and I were talking last night, Sandy," she began. "He thinks I am being unreasonable in not wanting you to go on that trip with your friends."

Sandy waited numbly.

"So I've finally decided that you can go with them if you want to."

The girl's eyes widened. "Do you mean it, Mom?"

"You can go with them or with Robert and me. I want you to make your choice."

"Oh, Mom!" Sandy kissed her impulsively. "Thank you! Thank you!"

Mrs. Fenwick pulled away slightly. "Then you are going to Alaska?" she asked.

"You said I could." Fear shadowed the girl's face. Maybe her mom had changed her mind.

"I said you could make your choice, and I'm going to live up to it. I don't mind telling you, though, that I am disappointed. I thought you would want to spend the summer with me."

"I do, Mom," Sandy blurted, "only the kids are all going to Alaska where they'll be working at a mission station and–" Her voice lost itself in silence. She knew it was hard for her mother to feel she was taking a backseat to a group of religious fanatics.

Sandy's getting to go North wasn't the only change of plans, however. Three days before they were to leave, the mission superintendent called Danny into his office.

"I've been doing a lot of thinking about the trip the kids of your church are taking. We'd like to do all we can to encourage it."

Danny still did not understand that Dr. Kroeger was doing more than making conversation, although he shared the feeling about the trip. His own interest in missions had first been ignited when he was a kid. He had visited the Mexican field where Kay's mother was a missionary. He always said he got a lifetime occupation and a wife out of that trip.

Dr. Kroeger picked up a pen and held it. "The station they'll be visiting is one of ours," he went on. "We're happy about that, too. I know there are a lot of different groups working in the North, but it's only natural that we'd be more concerned with the stations that are our responsibility."

Danny waited with growing curiosity. For the first time, he began to think the superintendent might have something else in mind.

"We've decided to ask you and Kay to go along with them, Danny. I'm sure you can be of service on the trip, and you might be able to help us pick up a few prospective missionaries."

Danny was stunned by Dr. Kroeger's request. He thanked him and left his office as quickly as possible to take the news to Kay. She would be as excited as he was.

Brenda Ekberg was the last to make up her mind to go. Everyone else had their bags packed and down to the garage where the bus was being loaded for the next day's departure before she approached Pastor Reeves hesitantly and asked if there would be room for her.

He studied her attractive young face. She was one of the newest Christians in the youth group, coming to Christ a few weeks before, sick of sin and longing for the peace forgiveness could bring. Since that time, her faith had blossomed. There was an earnestness in her life that was scarcely apparent in many kids who had been believers for several years.

When the trip was decided upon, Pastor Reeves was sure she would be one of the first to want to go and was disappointed when she didn't sign up. He had even talked with his wife about the advisability of going to see her in an effort to convince her that she should go with the others. Now, however, he had some reservations about her motives.

"Why do you want to go, Brenda?" he asked. "Is it because of the excitement and getting to see new places?"

"Oh, no, it isn't that at all," she replied quickly. She was disturbed that he would think that of her. "Actually, I'm not even sure I want to go. I mean, I wonder if I wouldn't rather stay at home." Her cheeks colored delicately. "What I mean is that I keep thinking how nice it would be to work this summer. Then I'd have money to buy clothes for school. I get to thinking about the missionaries in Alaska and what I could do to help, though." She stopped and gestured helplessly. "I'm not explaining myself very well."

"On the contrary, I think you've explained yourself very well indeed." A smile broke across his face. "I just wanted to be sure you weren't changing your mind because of the glamour of the trip."

# CHAPTER 2

# FIRST CRISIS

It was a happy, excited group that gathered in front of the church at dawn the first Saturday morning in June. Pastor Reeves led in prayer, asking God's watchful care over them before they boarded the bus. Sandy turned to DeeDee, who was sitting next to her.

"I can hardly believe it's true. I thought I was stuck going to LA this summer."

"It's almost a miracle the way God worked things out."

Danny, Mr. Cole, and Pastor Reeves alternated at the wheel of the big, cumbersome bus. The first day, they drove to Minot, North Dakota, turned north, and drove one hundred miles to Saskatchewan.

At night they stopped at one of the roadside campgrounds, pitched their tents, and cooked supper over propane camp stoves. Usually, there were other campers around by the time they had finished the evening meal and did their dishes. The second night on the highway, they decided to have a campfire service, and Danny asked Brenda if she would give her testimony.

"I don't know," she said. "I get so scared when I think about being in front of a lot of people that I'm afraid I won't even be able to make the words come out."

"You're with friends," he reminded her. "It shouldn't be so hard for you to tell the kids what God has done in your life."

Brenda frowned. It wasn't that she didn't want to. Ever since she made her decision to walk with Christ, she had wanted to do more for Him.

"I guess it wouldn't hurt to try."

A carload of girls drove in just as the campfire service was getting under way; and by the time Brenda's turn to speak came, they had wandered over, curious to see what was going on. She was so disturbed by the prospect of speaking in public that she was unaware of the fact that there were strangers in the group around the little fire.

"I'm not used to getting up before a crowd like this," she began. "I don't even know for sure what I–I ought to say; but it's like Danny told me, I should be glad for a chance to tell you what Jesus Christ did to straighten out the mess I'd made of my life."

The words dribbled off into silence, and, for a

moment, she looked around, as though trying to summon the courage to go on.

"Most of you know the kind of life I was leading only a year ago," she continued. "I was rebellious toward my parents and the authorities at school. In fact, I was rebellious toward anyone who tried to make me do anything I didn't want to do. I was determined to lead my own life."

Tears came to her eyes, and she wiped them away in embarrassment. "I did a lot of things that make me cringe when I think about them now, and I can't even imagine how bad my life would have been if I kept going the direction I was headed, but God wouldn't leave me alone. He kept dealing with me until I saw that I couldn't handle things on my own. If I didn't want to end up living the worst sort of life, I'd have to let Jesus Christ have complete control." She coughed nervously. "Now I've asked God's forgiveness, and it's really neat!"

She went on to explain how He had given purpose and direction to her life in spite of the hold sin had on her and how happy she was even at home, now that she was no longer rebellious.

There were several kids who were much more fluent than Brenda, but when she finished, a hush gripped the kids around the fire. Even after the pastor's wife closed in prayer, there was a time when no one spoke or moved. They broke up thoughtfully, still held by the meaning of the moment.

Brenda was about to go to the tent she shared with Sandy and DeeDee, when a youthful stranger approached and introduced herself. She appeared to be at least twenty-one years old.

"I'm Marty Ross," she said. "I'm with a couple of girlfriends on a camping trip to Alaska."

"We're glad to know you." Brenda introduced Sandy and DeeDee.

However, Marty wanted to talk only to Brenda. "You may not know it, but when you were talking, you sounded as though you were giving the story of my life."

Brenda smiled self-consciously. For a moment she wondered if the girl before her was a Christian too. "I guess there are a lot of us in that fix. And the answer's the same; we all need the Lord Jesus Christ."

Marty wrinkled her forehead. "You make it sound tempting, only I'm not a religious person."

"Neither am I. Actually, being a Christian isn't a matter of being religious. It's a life to live."

"I don't understand."

As Brenda continued talking to her, they walked some distance away from the others.

Marty seemed interested in what she heard. She had never seriously considered the fact that Jesus loved her so much that He died for her. She longed to feel that love.

Still, there were doubts.

"I don't think I could live up to it."

"You can't be what you ought to be in your own strength," Brenda told her. "None of us can. That's the reason we need Jesus Christ."

Marty wasn't sure she liked that. She knew she wasn't what she ought to be, but to have someone else say it wasn't exactly pleasing. "I don't follow you."

"If we could live the way we should without any help, there wouldn't have been any need for Jesus Christ to die on the cross for us," the other girl explained.

For almost an hour they talked. Brenda told her what it meant to fall in love with Jesus and to give her life completely to Him. Her new friend considered what she said and asked questions thoughtfully.

"If I could just understand it," she concluded, "but I don't get it at all."

"You're like I was when I first considered giving my heart and life to Jesus. You're trying to make it too difficult. The hard part is overcoming your own rebellious nature. Once you've decided you *want* Christ, the rest is easy. You tell Him you realize you need Him and thank Him for coming into your life. Tell Him that you know you're not what you ought to be and ask Him to give you a new life."

"You make it sound so easy."

"It is easy." Brenda was radiant. "It's the most wonderful thing in the whole world."

Marty was biting her nails. When her new friend talked about loving Jesus, she felt that she couldn't go on another day without Him. "Only you have to give up so much," she murmured reluctantly.

"It may sound like a Christian has to give up a lot," Brenda admitted, "but God changes your life until you don't even *want* to do some of the things that mean so much to you now." She would have said more, but Marty's weight shifted from one foot to the other almost imperceptibly, indicating her desire to end the conversation.

"I've got to think about it." With that she was gone.

Slowly Brenda made her way back to the tent.

"What happened?" DeeDee demanded eagerly. "Did she make a decision?"

"I'm afraid so." Brenda's voice sounded thick. "The trouble is, she didn't make the right one."

Before turning in that night, they knelt quietly and asked God to keep speaking to Marty until she was ready to let Him have His rightful place in her heart and life. When they finished, the night was broken only by the mournful whisper of the wind in the trees above.

"If we only were going to be with Marty for a few days," Sandy murmured, "you'd have another chance to talk to her."

"I'm going to see her again in the morning," Brenda said suddenly. "I have to make her understand that she can't put Jesus Christ off. She has to let Him come into her life."

She twisted restlessly in her sleeping bag. An hour

or more passed as she went over the conversation they would have the next morning, trying to anticipate the other girl's objections and find answers for them.

Brenda still had the uneasy feeling that she had failed both God and Marty. Almost anyone else would have been better able to talk to the other girl than she. If Danny had only asked DeeDee or Sandy or one of the others to speak, she might be a Christian by this time.

Kay would have known how to answer Marty's questions. She could have quoted Bible verses the girl could not have argued with. Brenda didn't know why she hadn't suggested that they go and talk with Kay.

She raised herself on one elbow, pensively. Kay would be willing to go with her to see Marty the next morning. She would waken Kay and ask her to go along. That was what she would do. Once the decision was made, sleep came almost immediately.

Brenda was up the next day before anyone else, tingling with excitement. Dressing quietly, she went out into the chilly morning air. She started for the Orlis tent some distance away, intent on waking Kay, but jerked to a halt.

Marty and her friends were gone! Only the matted grass where their tent had been revealed the fact that they had been there at all. They must have broken camp stealthily and left without waking anyone.

A feeling of nausea engulfed Brenda. Marty might never have another chance to become a Christian.

She wouldn't be able to talk with her again about her need of the Lord Jesus Christ. Great, tortured sobs shook her sagging shoulders.

Brenda's friends tried to comfort her, but she refused to listen. It was some time before she could stop crying long enough to help get breakfast and break camp.

The scenery that morning was breathtaking, but Brenda scarcely appreciated it. Her thoughts were with Marty, who had been seeking Christ but had chosen not to find Him. She knew now how those who tried to reach her for Christ must have felt when she was so stubborn.

* * *

They had been riding over the mountain trail for several hours that morning when the big bus hit a jagged rock and blew out a rear tire.

"Everybody out," Danny called jovially. "We've got some work to do."

"Just don't go too far," Brad added. "It's not going to take us long to get on the move again."

Pastor Reeves started to get the spare tire they had secured in the luggage rack on top of the bus, but it wasn't there. "Didn't we have a spare up here?"

"We sure did. I tied it there myself," Danny said.

"Well, it's gone." The minister touched the short length of rope that was still attached to the rack. The free end had been cut with a sharp knife. "Someone must have decided they needed it worse than we did."

"We can be thankful for the other spare," Brad put in. "Without it, we'd be in real trouble."

Danny didn't say anything, but he was still disturbed. He had flown over much of the North and knew that highway as well as though he had driven it. It was a good road but lived up to its reputation of being a killer on tires. They still had a long way to go before they reached a place big enough to carry a replacement. What if they had another blowout?

The girls walked along the road looking for unusual rocks, while the boys and the three men changed the tires. They loosened the lug bolts and were raising the wheel with the jack, when there was an ominous metallic *crack!* The wheel settled back on the gravel.

"What was that?" Brad demanded.

Pastor Reeves groaned aloud. "Take a look! It's our jack!"

# CHAPTER 3

# A THRILL FOR BRENDA

Conversation stopped suddenly, ripped apart in midsentence by the broken jack. Motion, too, was suspended, as though the weight that caused the trouble had, at the same time, robbed them all of the ability to act.

Pastor Reeves spoke first, woodenly. "What are we going to do?"

Brad, who had been loosening the bolts that held the wheel in place, straightened to stare up the long ribbon of rocks and gravel. "I guess we'll have to wait until a truck comes along and take our chances on stopping it to borrow a jack."

Only Danny Orlis was undisturbed. He had been born and raised in country like this, where a man had to use his own resourcefulness. "I don't think we'll have to wait for a truck," he said aloud. "Where did you put the ax, Brad?"

"What do you want with the ax?" Pastor Reeves asked.

"You'll see."

Brad got it for him. Danny started for the bush, motioning for Del and Doug and several others to go along. "I'm going to need a little muscle," he explained.

A few minutes later, they came back to the road carrying a long pole. Del and Doug had a short section of log about a foot in diameter.

Danny had the boys put the short log on the roadbed about a foot behind the axle. Then, shoving one end of the long pole under the truck and using the short log as a fulcrum, they raised the wheel.

"It'll have to go a little higher," Danny said.

Two others added their weight to that on the pole. That was enough to give them the clearance they needed to remove the flat and put on the spare. They were tightening the last lug bolt when a truck that was also headed north pulled up behind them and stopped.

"Trouble?" the driver asked as he leaned out the window.

"Everything's under control now," Danny answered.

The young trucker grinned. "Fine. Just thought I'd check." He shifted gears, and the monstrous vehicle passed the bus and began to creep up the hill.

Brad crawled behind the wheel and honked the horn to summon the girls back to the bus. Everyone piled in, and they were about ready to continue their journey when another bus roared noisily past them.

"Whoever those guys are, they're in an awful hurry."

"That's the same rig that passed us yesterday," Del said. "They've got it fixed up as a camper."

Doug noticed that the bus was the same as theirs, but he was thinking of something else. "You don't suppose those birds are the ones who stole our tire and wheel?"

"Could be," Danny replied, "but there are a lot of people who might be interested in a tire that size. Think what it could be sold for up here."

About a dozen miles ahead, they crossed a narrow, turbulent river. On the other side of the bridge, the converted camper bus was stopped, and the men in it were hastily setting up their fishing tackle. Doug turned to Danny.

"Why don't we stop and see if those guys have our tire?"

"We can't do that."

The boy still was not satisfied. "Why not? We could camp beside them so we could snoop around a little."

He was still grumbling because they didn't stop when they finally came to a campground that suited the others. As they slowed down to pull into the camping area, Brenda's eyes lit up.

"Look who's here!" She pointed a quavering finger at the car that belonged to Marty and her two girlfriends. They must have stopped some time earlier, because they had already made camp and were cooking supper over an open fire. "This morning I didn't think I would ever see her again!"

As soon as the bus stopped, Brenda got out and went over to the camp of Marty and her companions. The other girl came to greet her. "This is something of a coincidence. I didn't think we would ever get to see each other again."

"I don't know much about things like this," Brenda answered, "but I really don't think it was a coincidence at all."

A strange look came into Marty's eyes. "Come again? I don't think I understand you."

"A coincidence is something that just happens, and I don't think this just happened. I think it's an answer to prayer that we met here tonight."

The other girl's smile vanished. She didn't know whether she was ready to accept what Brenda said or not, but it bothered her.

"I laid awake for the longest time last night trying to think of what to say to you when I went over to see you this morning, but you were gone."

"I sort of figured you were planning on talking to me," Marty said honestly. "That was the reason I got the other girls up so early this morning and insisted on breaking camp before we had breakfast. I wanted to be sure we got away before you woke up."

Brenda was hurt. "You mean you didn't want to see me again?"

"It wasn't that at all." Marty was nervously fumbling for words. "I was afraid I couldn't hold out for a second time."

This, Brenda was able to understand. "I was the same way before I made my decision for Christ," she went on, keeping her voice down so the others would not overhear. "I couldn't get away fast enough from the first person who presented Jesus Christ to me."

The haunting cry of a loon echoed in the still air.

Brenda continued, "I thought I could run away from Christ, but I soon found that I couldn't. In the next few days, He went with me every place I went. It didn't make any difference where I was or what I was doing, Jesus Christ and the fact that I was a sinner and lost unless I allowed Him to take away my sin and give me a new life were all I could think about."

Marty nodded. "That's exactly the way I felt. Last night I didn't sleep at all, and this morning I knew I *had* to get away from you. I couldn't risk talking to you again – even though I really wanted to." She paused. "Tell me, honestly. Did it really make so much difference in your life when you became a Christian?"

Brenda nodded quickly. "It made such a difference that, looking back, I can hardly believe I was ever the old Brenda Ekberg. Jesus Christ gave me an entirely new life." She moved closer. "And He can do the same for you if you will only let Him."

Marty could resist no longer. "And how do I do that?"

The other girl did not answer immediately. She wasn't going to make the same mistake she had made the night before. This time she would get help.

"Let's talk to Kay," she suggested. "She can explain it so much better than I can."

However, Marty did not move. "I don't want to talk to her. I want to talk to you."

Brenda's lips trembled, and she stared hesitantly at Marty. She wanted to help her new friend, but she wasn't sure she could do it. It had been such a short time before that she herself had made that same decision. Besides, she felt awkward witnessing to someone almost five years older than she.

"I'm so new at this. I don't know all the answers."

"You know what you did to become a Christian, don't you?"

Brenda nodded. This wasn't the way Brenda planned on doing it, but she had no choice. Marty refused to talk with anyone else. So she said, "First, the pastor read some Bible verses that showed me I was a sinner. Then he read some that showed me that Jesus Christ is the answer to the problem of sin and all my other problems." As Brenda talked, she prayed desperately that God would help her to say things in a way that Marty could understand. "Finally, I saw that I could be a Christian and have an entirely new life if I would just confess my sin and let Jesus Christ take complete charge of me and everything I thought or did or wanted to do."

"I just remembered I used to hear something like that when I went to Sunday school as a little girl, but that's been a long time ago. I hadn't heard anything like it since until last night when you told what Jesus has done in your life."

"I'd never gone to church much either." Brenda's face lit. "And I don't know the Bible well enough even to remember where to find those verses the pastor read to me, but I can tell you that I have a new life in Jesus. There isn't any doubt about that. And for the first time since I can remember, I have been truly happy. Oh, I still have problems. I'd be lying to you if I tried to tell you that I don't. But I have the assurance that God will help me if I call on Him. And, Marty, you can have the same new life if you will turn your old life over to Jesus Christ and walk with Him!"

Tears flooded the other girl's eyes and trickled hotly down her cheeks. "I want it, Brenda!" she exclaimed, her voice breaking. "I want exactly what you have."

The two girls bowed their heads, and Brenda helped Marty pray, thanking God for accepting her into His family. They also asked for courage for Marty to make a complete break with the bad in her life and to let Christ be Himself through her.

By the time they got back to the bus, camp was set up, and supper was almost ready.

Sandy saw them approaching and hurried over to

them. "Oh, there you are. I was beginning to wonder what happened to you. We're about ready to eat."

Brenda smiled. "I think Marty has something to tell you."

Her companion colored slightly. "–I–" She stared at Brenda in bewilderment. "I don't know what to say."

"Why don't you tell Sandy what happened?"

Marty swallowed hard against the sudden lump in her throat. "I decided I was tired of living my old life," she began, the words tripping over her tongue. "I–I asked Jesus to save me, and He gave me a new life, like Brenda has."

Sandy's face glowed. "Oh, that's wonderful!"

By this time, it seemed that half the members of the church group had gathered around and were listening. Kay and Mrs. Reeves introduced themselves to the girl and expressed their own pleasure at what had happened. For more than half an hour, the two women talked with Marty and Brenda, going over the plan of salvation step by step, to be sure the new Christian understood exactly what she had done. Before the conversation was over, they gave the new convert a Bible and outlined a plan for starting her personal Bible study.

"And we want you to know that we'll all be praying for you every day," Kay assured her.

Marty smiled graciously. "Thank you so much." Then her expression changed. "I've been looking forward to this trip to Alaska all year, but to be honest with you I didn't know that something was going to happen even before we got there that would change my entire life."

Brenda was so excited over what had happened that she could scarcely sleep that night. She was wide awake when Sandy and DeeDee opened their eyes the next morning, and while they were taking down the tent, her experience with Marty was all she could talk about.

"I used to think I had exciting times when I was living for myself," she said, "but nothing I did then can even compare with the joy and excitement I had last night when I was able to help Marty make her decision."

"I don't know that I can blame you for it," Sandy said. "I'd give a lot if I could help someone like you did."

"To think I almost stayed at home."

DeeDee thought about that. "I wonder how many times we miss being a real blessing to someone else because we don't do what God wants us to."

The next two days of the trip were very much like the first days on the highway. They were still on the graveled portion of the road and were playing leap-frog with the camper bus. The converted bus would usually go roaring past them sometime between breakfast and noon. Later in the afternoon, they would pass the bus stopped along a stream or lake.

"I wonder why those guys don't make any better

time than they do," Doug said. "They drive so much faster than we do, they pass us as though we're standing still."

"You saw them back at the river," Danny reminded him. "They drive fast so they can stop and fish for a while."

The next morning the bus came blasting up behind them as fast as usual, blowing the horn for them to make room on the narrow graveled road. Pastor Reeves, who was driving at the time, edged closer to the shoulder but not fast enough to satisfy the driver of the vehicle behind. He blared on the horn again and swerved to pass them.

Del, who was sitting on the outside, saw how close the other vehicle was and shuddered. "Those guys aren't giving us any room!" he exclaimed.

Pastor Reeves tightened his grip on the steering wheel and moved carefully away from the converted bus that was edging ever closer to them. Suddenly there was a report like that of a high-powered rifle. The bus lurched dangerously! Someone in the back screamed! And Pastor Reeves fought to keep control of the careening vehicle!

# CHAPTER 4

# UNEXPECTED RESCUE

The heavy bus lurched wildly as the tire blew and they teetered along the edge of the steep slope. A wordless prayer went up as Pastor Reeves battled against the relentless pull of the wheel. Gradually, after what seemed to be an eternity but was only moments, the bus slowed. And as it did, he was able to inch it back onto the heavily graveled road.

At last it jerked to a halt. The engine died, and all was silent. For at least a minute, no one spoke or moved. Then Pastor Reeves half turned in the seat.

"We should thank God for protecting us," he murmured. "It was only His grace that kept us from going over the edge."

Danny paled as he looked out the bus window. "You can say that again."

The minister asked Brad to lead them in prayer, and only after he finished praying did anyone get up.

Del and Doug looked at the blown out front tire and back at the mountain slope they had almost gone over. "Take a look at those tracks right along the edge, Doug. I'll bet we couldn't do that again without going over!"

Doug brushed his hand across his sweat-beaded forehead. "It gives me the shakes just to think about it."

Pastor Reeves, who had crawled out on the other side of the bus, walked around to the front and approached Brad Cole. "I'll go and cut another pole if you want to get the spare out and start loosening the lug bolts."

Brad frowned. "What spare?"

The men stared at each other. From time to time it had bothered them that they were driving without a spare. They had even stopped at every service station along the road to see if they could buy an extra tire, but they had not been unduly concerned when they were unable to get one. After all, the rest of the tires were good. Now, however, the full import of their situation became apparent to them.

The minister glanced back at the young people who were milling uncertainly around the bus and lowered his voice. "This is a bad deal, Danny. What are we going to do?"

Danny picked up a pebble and threw it off the road to keep from having to answer immediately. It *was* a bad deal. They had a busload of people and a limited amount of food, and the chances were that there wasn't another tire within a hundred miles of where they were. They knew there wasn't anything south. They had stopped at every possible place in an effort to buy a tire.

"We'll have to have someone catch a ride to one of the service stations north and see what we can find."

Pastor Reeves nodded. "I suppose you're right, but I don't see how we can expect anyone north of us to have the size tire we need. Nobody south had anything that would even come close."

The Davis boys came up in time to hear what the minister had said. "Do you think we can find a bus tire way out here, Danny?" Doug asked uneasily.

"God has a tire somewhere for us. I'm convinced of that."

Pastor Reeves and Brad Cole were looking at a map with Danny to see how far it was to the next service station when Marty and her two friends stopped to see what was wrong. Their car was small, but they insisted that Danny ride with them. He got in their car, and they pulled away.

"I wish Danny didn't have to leave," DeeDee told Sandy. "I feel uneasy when he's gone."

"But Dad and Pastor Reeves are here."

"And so is God," Brenda added.

The girls Danny Orlis was riding with had only driven a few miles when they saw the converted camper bus stopped beside a fast-running stream.

"Isn't that bus about the same as yours?" Marty asked.

Danny's eyes gleamed hopefully. "They just might have an extra tire we could buy."

They pulled into the camping area and stopped, and he went over to where one of the men was fishing.

"I'm from the bus you've been passing at least once a day since we left Edmonton," Danny said by way of introduction.

"So?" There was a sneer in the man's voice.

Danny told him they had blown a tire, omitting the fact that their bus had forced Pastor Reeves to the edge of the road, causing him to hit a rock that cut the casing.

"What do you expect us to do about it?"

By this time the other two men had joined them.

"I thought you might have an extra tire we could use until we get some place where we can buy a new one."

"Sorry," the fisherman retorted curtly. "We can't help you."

"We've got two spares," one of the others said.

"We might need them both."

"But this guy's stranded with a busload of kids, Russ. We ought to help him if we can."

"What do you expect me to do, cry about it?" He turned away. "They got into this mess. Let 'em get out of it the best way they can."

Danny tried to reason with him, but it was apparent

that talking would do no good. The stranger had already made up his mind. Danny thanked them and went back to the car, dejection pulling at his heels and sagging his shoulders.

The girls were indignant when they learned what had happened. "I've never heard of anything so selfish," Marty said.

Danny changed the subject.

Back on the highway where the bus was stalled, the hours dragged endlessly. The sun seemed to hang motionless in the sky, and the shadows refused to move. At first the pastor and Brad tried to make themselves believe Danny would be able to get a tire at the nearest service station and would soon be back with it, but, as time passed, they began to doubt that he would be back that day.

"We'd better get our gear carried over to that little clearing and start putting up the tents," Pastor Reeves suggested.

"Good idea," Brad replied.

Some of the group protested, however. They thought they ought to give Danny a chance to return before setting up camp.

"If he does get back in an hour or so, we might want to drive on a little farther tonight," Doug said.

"Yeah," Del agreed. "I bet we could finish Alberta and pick up the Alaska Highway in Dawson Creek before dark."

Pastor Reeves shook his head, and Brad agreed

that it was wise for them to make camp in plenty of time before dark.

While the boys were gathering wood and pitching the tents, DeeDee and Sandy gathered the girls together and held another impromptu prayer meeting.

At long last the sun slipped from its cloudless stronghold above and rested on the rim of the western hills. It would not be long until it ducked out of sight and darkness would close in once more around the bus. The little group tried to ignore it, however.

The tents were set up, the firewood was cut, and the water was carried from the nearby stream. Those who weren't cooking were gathered in little clusters, talking about the latest crisis.

Kay busied herself with supper and tried not to think about Danny being gone or the bewildering situation in which they found themselves. He was the logical choice to have gone after the new tire, she had to agree. He knew the North much better than the others did, and he was resourceful. If anyone could find the spare they needed so desperately, he could. She couldn't help being uneasy, but she hoped her concern didn't show.

Brad sauntered over to his daughter's tent. Sandy and Brenda were chatting about the trip and what they would do in Alaska. When Sandy saw her dad, she excused herself. The two of them strolled away from the camp.

"I suppose you're wishing you'd gone to Los Angeles with your mother about now," Brad commented.

"Oh, no." Her answer was quick and firm. "I wouldn't want to miss any of this. It's been wonderful."

"Even the trouble?"

"Even the trouble." Her smile winked at him. "God will help us."

"I know that," he said, hoping he sounded less concerned than he really was. "When we get home, I suppose this is one of the things we'll laugh about."

They walked a little distance into the woods together, their arms intertwined.

"It's so wonderful being with you, Dad. I wish we could be together like this always."

"So do I."

She turned quickly. "Can't we?"

He stared at her. "Sandy, don't even talk like that." His voice was harsh with emotion.

"Mom has Robert. She doesn't need me. Why can't we be together?"

He glanced at his watch. "It's getting late, Sandy. We'd better get back and help with the work."

Sandy said no more about it, but the seed lay in a fertile corner of her mind. Maybe they could work things out so she could live with her dad and keep house for him. That was all she could think about as they rejoined the others.

They were about ready to eat their evening meal when a huge semitrailer truck coming from the north pulled over beside the disabled bus and stopped. The gangling driver got out and waved to them. "Time for supper?"

Pastor Reeves recognized him as the same trucker who stopped a few days before when they had their first blowout. He had been headed north then; now he must be returning home.

"Come and join us," the pastor invited.

"Don't mind if I do."

"I'm Pastor Reeves. We're from Fairview, Minnesota."

"Pleased to meet you, sir. I'm Hank Morgen from no place special. Right now I'm on my way to Chicago."

Pastor Reeves introduced Hank to Brad and the kids standing close by. Hank noticed the food on the campfire. "That sure looks good." He turned to the minister and Brad. "Do you always eat like this?"

"We will for a while, anyway. But if Danny doesn't get back soon, we may not."

"What's the trouble?"

Pastor Reeves explained about the blowout and the tire situation.

"So Danny caught a ride with a car going north," Brad put in. "He was going to the nearest service station to buy a tire, but he hasn't come back yet."

"He's not going to find a tire to fit your rig this side of Dawson Creek, and he might not be able to get one there," Hank said, shaking his head.

Pastor Reeves knew the situation was serious. Hank's attitude confirmed it.

"You've got an out-of-the-ordinary size tire on your bus," Hank continued. "It's not going to be easy to find a place this far north that stocks one like it."

Brad and the minister stared at one another, the color draining from their cheeks.

The pastor replied, "Humanly speaking, that's real bad; but we have to remember that there's nothing too hard for the Lord."

Hank's mouth tightened, and then he spoke. "You sound as though you really believe that," he said skeptically.

"I do. I've seen God answer prayer more times than I can remember."

The young newcomer shrugged. "Well, if it makes you feel any better, I won't knock it; but I can tell you this much, I'd a lot rather have the help of a good, well-stocked tire store right now, if I were you, than this help of the Lord you talk about."

It was then that Mrs. Reeves called them to supper.

Before they ate, the pastor led them in prayer. "Lord, You know about the trouble we've been having and how scarce tires are the size we need. We don't know where Danny is or what success he's having, but we're trusting you to guide him to the place where he can find a tire that will fit our bus. Now, Lord, bless this food and us to Your service–" and everyone murmured, "Amen." They were still eating when Hank turned to Pastor Reeves. "I passed a camping area ten miles up the road where a camper bus had stopped for the night. If I remember right, it's a bus about like this one. They just might have a spare tire and wheel."

"We know about them."

"The fact is," Brad said, "They are the guys who crowded us off the road and caused us to have the blowout."

Hank's face darkened. "I've been passed by guys like that a few times myself." When he finished eating, he stood and stretched. "Now, if you'll help me get this trailer unhooked, I'll go back and talk to them about that tire."

Brad and Pastor Reeves stared at him. This was something neither had expected.

It wasn't long until the trucker came back. Even before he stopped, they saw the tire and wheel tied to the tractor frame.

Hardly before the truck was completely stopped, he opened the door and climbed out. He beamed triumphantly. "I told you I'd get it, didn't I?" he asked, noting the astonishment on their faces.

The young people and their sponsors could scarcely believe they now had the tire they needed. A couple of girls started to cry their relief.

"This is one time you won't be able to thank God," Hank said. *I'm* the one who helped you out of the mess."

Pastor Reeves smiled. "We do appreciate your help, Hank, but who do you think sent you along at this particular time? Did you ever wonder about that?"

The young trucker stared at him incredulously. "As a matter of fact, I've wondered plenty about it. I was going to lay over for a couple of days in Dawson Creek," he said, "but at the last minute, I decided to pull out. And I didn't know why."

"Now you know."

"If we can get that tire on your bus," Hank said, changing the subject suddenly, "I'll be on my way."

Brad was standing at the back of the tractor, loosening the wire that held the tire and wheel in place.

"This wheel looks familiar."

"It should." Hank laughed dryly. "It used to belong to you. Your friends in the camper bus are the same guys who stole your spare."

Brad and the minister shook their heads in disbelief. "How did you get them to tell you that?"

He grinned mysteriously. "Let's say I had a hunch and did a little persuading."

With the truck jack, changing the tire was only a matter of minutes. When they finished and had helped their benefactor get his semitrailer hooked up to the tractor, he was ready to leave.

"I really wasn't so smart in dealing with those guys. They acted suspicious when I pressed them about selling me a tire and wheel, so I snooped around a bit. The instant I saw that wheel and realized it was painted the same color as your bus, I remembered what you told me about having a tire stolen, and I jumped them about it. They weren't going to admit it until I said I was going to radio for the RCMP and have them all arrested." His laughter echoed over the still air. "They realized I meant it and got real nice about giving it to me."

Hank climbed back into his truck and leaned out the window. "By the way," he continued. "I told them you wouldn't have them arrested if you got your tire and wheel back. Okay?"

# CHAPTER 5

# SAFE ARRIVAL

The young people and their sponsors were silent, watching the huge truck until it rumbled out of sight behind a cloud of dust. When the trucker was gone Doug turned to Brad. "Hank's a great guy, isn't he?"

"You can say that again."

"There aren't many who'd stop and help us the way he did."

"He is a nice guy," Sandy's dad said, "but I'm sure God caused him to stop and do what he did."

Doug nodded his agreement. It was strange how things worked out as far as their stolen tire and wheel were concerned and that they were able to get it back when they needed it.

"Why do you suppose God let that happen?" the boy wanted to know.

Brad shrugged. "We never know why God does or

doesn't do certain things. I don't think we even have the right to ask the question. Of course, He might have allowed them to steal our tire so He could get it back to us and teach us that we're to depend on Him."

Doug thought about that. They had been taught by Danny and Kay to look to God to help them work out every problem, but there were times when it seemed foolish, as though they didn't have to depend on Him, they could take care of themselves.

Brad looked over at his daughter. There were so many times when he felt he couldn't carry on, especially after Sandy's mother married someone else and he realized there was no chance of their ever getting back together again. It was situations like this that taught him that God does care and was looking after him.

Kay Orlis and some of the others wanted to break camp and go on that evening, at least as far as the service station where Danny was going for a tire. Pastor Reeves and Brad, however, thought it better to spend the night where they were.

"It's been a long day for all of us, and we're terribly tired," the minister said. "We need a night's rest before we hit the road again."

Brad added, "We can get up early in the morning and be on our way."

Kay was sure she would not sleep at all that night, but after the campfire service, which became a praise and prayer meeting, she was able to crawl into her sleeping bag and go right to sleep. God had taken care of them in such a wonderful way regarding the near disaster and the tire. He would take care of Danny too, wherever he was. The next morning Kay was the most calm and relaxed person of the group as they finished breakfast and began to take down the tents.

They drove on to the next service station, which was an hour's drive past the place where Hank had said he had found the camper bus. They all looked for it as they went by, but it was not to be seen.

"I suppose those guys were afraid we'd turn them in to the authorities if we saw them again," Del said.

"Maybe so. Anyway, they're gone," his brother added.

At the service station, they stopped and talked with the attendant. The bus, he said, had gone by late the night before. No, it hadn't stopped. However, Danny had stopped the afternoon before, asking about a big tire.

"I was real sorry, but we didn't have a thing that he could use," the man said with genuine regret.

Kay spoke up. "Did he say where he was going or what he was going to do?"

"He went on to Dawson Creek, but I doubt that he'd find anything there."

The kids in the bus looked at one another curiously. They were beginning to see the scope of what God had done for them in providing the tire. The situation would have been critical if it hadn't been for Hank Morgen.

They went on to Dawson Creek, British Columbia, and found Danny canvassing the places that might have tires.

"Am I ever glad to see you guys!" he exclaimed, hurrying up to the group. "I was beginning to wonder if we were ever going to get the bus up here. What happened? How did you manage?"

Pastor Reeves did not answer him immediately. "Did you find a tire?"

"Not yet, but there's a service station north of here quite some distance that has one. We contacted them by radio and found out for sure. They're going to send it down on the first truck that goes by. Now, how did you get up here?"

They all looked at Brad Cole, silently making him their spokesman. He was all too glad to be the one to tell Danny the great news. "I've heard you and Pastor Reeves tell how God answered your prayers at different times, but I'll have to be honest with you; I hadn't seen much of that myself. Now I know what God does for Christians who call on Him for help. It's things like this that can change a person's whole life." And then he related the rest of the story of their unexpected rescue.

Two days later, Hank Morgen, still headed south, switched on his radio to a clear-channel country music station. Ever since he talked with that preacher and his friends, he had been thinking about them. Some people on the highway were too stupid to know when they were in a jam; they didn't know enough to be worried. The men in charge of the bus weren't that way. They realized they were in a tough spot, but they weren't panicking. They acted as though they really believed what they said about God's taking care of them. The women and kids believed it too. They didn't seem to be all upset by what had happened.

As for himself, Hank had never had much use for religion. The way he looked at it, religion was all right for women and kids who didn't know any better or for people who were too old to think about anything except the grave. But this bunch was different. They were intelligent and had properly planned their trip North. He sure wouldn't have picked any of them as the kind he'd have figured would be associated with religion. That was what threw him.

The radio announcer gave the news and weather, and Hank's attention was drawn away from the group in the bus. Then a song came on that he had heard numerous times before and had always switched off.

This time, however, he listened curiously. The speaker began, and, as he talked, Hank listened so intently, his speed fell off about ten miles an hour. He couldn't quite understand what the guy on the radio was talking about, but he had the feeling it was something a lot like the things that preacher had said to him just before he left.

When the program was over, a raucous singing group took its place. Usually, he listened to that sort of music – not because he particularly liked it, but because it dispelled the feeling that he was alone. This particular night, however, it jarred him; so he turned it off. He had some serious things to think about. The papers and the little booklet the preacher gave him were stuffed in his pocket. Actually, he hadn't intended to read the stuff at all, but he had liked the preacher and hadn't wanted to hurt his feelings. Now, he decided he would read that stuff when he stopped. Talking to the preacher back on the road and listening to the guy on the radio touched a responsive chord in his heart, a longing he had often felt but didn't know why. It just might be that this was the something he needed, something that would give purpose and direction to his life.

* * *

At Dawson Creek, they began driving on the Alaska (Alcan) Highway. This highway took them all the way to Palmer, Alaska. The rest of the trip, through the Yukon and on to Palmer, was made by the Fairview church group without further difficulty. They went through the fertile Matanuska River valley, into Palmer, where they picked up their mail and drove out to the mission station some fifty miles east of the Alaskan community.

The superintendent, Bob Kline, enthusiastically greeted them. He was a massive, towering individual, with broad shoulders and hands like hams. His smile was contagious.

"I'll show you to your cabins, and, after you've had a chance to get settled and freshen up, we'll have a look around."

"Sounds great," Danny told him. "We're anxious to see where we'll be working."

"You might not be so anxious to see it when you find out all the jobs we've got lined up. There's plenty to do, and then some."

All of the young guys carried the luggage out of the bus and into the rooms the mission was providing for them. Sandy and Brenda were going to be together in one room, but DeeDee asked if they could move in another cot so she could be with them.

"That's all right with me," the superintendent said, "if you think there's enough room."

Del and Doug were to share a room. "I'm glad we're together," Del said. "If there are just the two of us together, we'll have a better chance of getting acquainted with some of the Inuit and Indian kids, and that's what I want to do."

When they finished carrying the luggage into the quarters they would be using, they left the bus and walked to the end of the long building so they could get an unobstructed view of the mountains.

"Wow!" Doug exclaimed. "How would you like

to get caught in a blizzard at the top of one of those ridges?"

Del shuddered. "I wouldn't care to be up on one of those mountains at all, even if there wasn't a blizzard."

The mission station was, indeed, located in a breathtakingly beautiful spot. The buildings were nestled in a jewel-like valley along a frothing mountain stream. On either side, sheer granite cliffs thrust upward to the snow-shrouded mountaintops.

"Oo-ee!" Doug exclaimed. "I'm going to like it here!"

# CHAPTER 6

# PULLING DOUG'S LEG

The missionary, Bob Kline, took Danny, Brad, and Pastor Reeves on a brief tour of the mission station that evening after dinner, showing them the buildings they all would be working on. There was a great deal for them to do, that was true. There was a school to build, new roofs to be put on two other buildings, and some remodeling to take care of.

"It looks as if we've tried to find everything we could for you to do, but it seems like we never have enough hands or hours in the day to do all the work that needs to be done," Bob said. "Anything you can do will be a big help to us."

Danny nodded. He spent much of his time on various mission stations and heard the same plea everywhere. "We've got our work cut out for us," he replied.

"That's for sure," Brad put in.

The mission superintendent took them into the office where he had the plans for the new school building.

"This is our biggest project. If we get this new school built while you're here, we'll be able to double its capacity. It has our number one priority."

"I'm surprised at that," Pastor Reeves said. "I would have thought a new church or perhaps a hospital would be more important."

"Indian parents are more anxious to have their kids educated today. If we can provide the space for them, we'll have plenty of new kids to fill it." He paused. "Every new student is another opportunity to reach a family for Christ."

The rest of the group was as anxious as the men to see the mission station, but by the time they were settled in their rooms and had washed the grime of the gravel road away, it was time for dinner. Afterward, everyone was so tired, they decided it would be better to wait until the next day.

"We'll show you around here first," Bob Kline said. "Then we'll split into smaller groups and visit some of the villages in the area, so you can meet some of the people and see how they live."

The girls looked forward to visiting the villages. It was all they had been able to talk about when they were in their room the night before.

"I saw a little Inuit baby last night," Brenda

exclaimed, her face glowing. "He was the cutest, most darling little boy I've ever seen."

"They are cute," Sandy said, walking to the window and looking out. "Maybe we'll get a chance to help take care of some of those babies before we go back home. Dad said he thought we might be doing some babysitting so the mothers could take part in several days of Bible study."

DeeDee breathed deeply. "That would be too good to be true. I'll probably wind up helping Doug and Del do carpenter work or scrubbing floors or washing dishes. That's about the way things usually go. I get stuck with something that isn't much fun."

Brenda Ekberg turned to face her companions, deliberately. There was a softness in her face that neither of them had ever seen before. "This is going to sound funny to you," she said, "because you both know how selfish I've been, but I really don't care what kind of work I'm asked to do. All I care about is doing something for the mission that might help someone to make a decision for Christ or to grow in faith so he can do a better job of serving Him."

DeeDee was sorry she had been complaining. "You make me ashamed of myself, Brenda. I guess I feel the same as you do, only I forgot it for a minute."

At breakfast that morning, Sandy was unusually quiet, listening to the conversation of the Klines' fellow missionaries. The talk centered on a current outreach for Christ in the community. It seemed to

Sandy that these people must never have any personal problems; their only concern was reaching people with the gospel of Jesus Christ.

Even the kids she came North with had no real difficulties, she thought, not compared to hers, at least. She had to live with her mother in a home where Jesus Christ wasn't honored. Her mother was a good person and so was her stepfather; only they didn't have any time for God. If they were sitting at one of the tables right now, they would be thinking they had never heard anything so ridiculous in their lives. They just didn't understand. That was one of the things that made living a Christian life so hard. That, and the fact that every time she saw her mom and Robert together, a knife twisted in her heart.

Sandy looked across the room at her dad who was enjoying his conversation with Bob. She didn't see how he could laugh at all. She knew he felt even worse than she did. She began to feel very sorry for herself. She had to live with her mother and Robert when her dad was all alone.

Sandy had done a lot of thinking since she and her dad had had that talk a few days before. He needed her; there wasn't any question about that. He had to work all day and come home to clean his apartment and cook and wash at night. His shirts were always a little wrinkled, and his apartment wasn't as clean as it ought to be. He needed someone to look after him.

Living with her dad would be wonderful. Now

that he was a Christian, they could study the Bible and pray and go to church together. It would be a lot easier to live the way a Christian should if they were together. They could help each other.

Sandy didn't know why the judge could decide where she had to live. She wasn't a little kid anymore. In a couple of years she would be able to vote. That ought to give her some rights about where she lived. Somehow, she was going to get that changed. Shortly after breakfast, Bob split the youth group into smaller parties and assigned missionaries to take them out to the villages. The girls were in the party led by his wife, Patti, a slight, bubbling brunette, who looked little older than they did. She drove expertly over the rough trail and crossed a small creek on a bridge that seemed destined to collapse before they got to the other side.

The village they visited was snuggled in the shadow of the mountain, a collection of shacks scattered carelessly along the shore of the small lake, with all the abandon of marbles rolled from a sack. Patti stopped before they reached the settlement.

"Well?" There was a question in her voice.

DeeDee's eyes widened. The houses, if they could be called that, were inexpertly hammered together from the materials at hand. Some were made of logs laid one against the other without benefit of plane or ax to narrow the cracks and help keep out the cold. They had been liberally chinked with moss, but that had been long ago. Much of it had dried and fallen out in winters past. Other houses were built of boards sawed from green timber that had warped and cracked with age. The glass was broken out of most of the windows, and cardboard or plywood was tacked over the openings.

Skinny, ragged youngsters with matted hair and dirt on their hands and faces were playing near one of the houses. While the visitors watched, a woman as grimy as the kids, hobbled out the door and around the corner of the house, yelling something DeeDee and her companions did not understand. When she turned, they saw a cigarette dangling loosely from her lips.

"I wouldn't have believed it," DeeDee murmured, doubt edging her voice. "If I hadn't actually seen her come out of that old shack, I wouldn't have believed anyone could possibly live in a place like that."

The smile was gone from Patti Kline's usually happy features. "I don't mind telling you it still shocks me to see some of the houses people around here live in, and we've been here long enough that I ought to be used to it."

Brenda spoke up quickly. "Nobody would live in a place like that in the *winter*, would they?"

"But they do," Patti answered quickly. "I think that's the hardest thing for me to see. The government has built some new homes for the Inuit, and they're building more all the time; but there are still so very many who have to live in places like this. It's bad enough to have to be in a shack like this in the summer, but to see them suffering through a bitter Northern winter in such a place is almost more than I can stand." There were tears in her eyes.

"There must be a lot of sickness," Brenda murmured.

"Every family has its case of TB, and every year people die of pneumonia."

At last Sandy spoke. "Isn't there anything more that can be done?"

"We try," Patti answered. "The people have to be taught to have pride in their homes and to learn how to take care of them when they do get a new house. That isn't always easy when you realize they have never before lived in a place that would need to be taken care of. It's not enough just to lead them to Christ. We have to go to work on other things as well."

With that, she started the engine once more and drove into the village. After walking among the shacks for half an hour and going into some of them, Patti took them back to the mission station. The girls said little until they got back to the mission station where they would be staying for the next nine weeks.

"You haven't told me what you think," Patti said to the girls. "You haven't said anything since we left the village."

Brenda was the spokesman. "I think we're all a little stunned by what we've seen today. I know I had no idea there was such a great need for everything."

She paused. "A person wouldn't even know where to start."

"You're right about that. The need is so great, it would be easy to get discouraged. There are times when we feel we aren't accomplishing anything and we might as well quit. Then the Lord gives us encouragement when a boy or girl or a mother or father trusts in Him. Then we realize again that it really is worth everything."

Sandy laughed, and her companions stared at her.

"I didn't think there was anything to laugh at," DeeDee observed curtly.

"I'm sorry. I was just thinking that my idea of being a missionary was so different than what it really is. I always thought of it as being glamorous and romantic. I figured the people all loved the missionaries so much and were so glad they had come to bring them the gospel that the missionaries would never be discouraged."

"I wish that were true," Patti replied. "I wouldn't trade our life here for any other anywhere in the world. It's interesting and it is rewarding. Believe me, it is. It isn't glamorous or romantic, though, and there are times when it gets very discouraging."

Bob was anxious to have the visitors begin the work. There was so much to do and so few days to do it in, but he thought they might want to rest for a couple of days and do some fishing and hiking before getting to work. Pastor Reeves and Danny had other ideas, however.

"When the kids indicated they wanted to come, we made it plain that this wasn't to be a vacation. We came up here to work, and the sooner we begin, the more we'll finish before we have to go back," Danny said.

"Well, you're not going to get any argument from me on that score. We're ready to start whenever you are."

They divided the group into smaller crews and placed them under the direction of the more experienced men. Some were used on the new school building, the rest were needed for repair work and inside finishing on one of the houses. Del and Doug were set to reroofing one of the places a new missionary couple lived in. Sandy and DeeDee helped tape the wallboard that had been installed previously. When that was done, they were to paint the walls and lay tile in the kitchen. Some of the girls washed windows and scrubbed woodwork, and a couple were even put to helping Doug and Del nail roofing.

The boys complained about it, but it didn't do any good.

"A couple of girls!" Del's lips curled in derision. "That's crazy! When they get done, I suppose we'll have to do the whole job over."

"I'll have you know I've helped with this job

before," Brenda informed them. "I can nail shingles as well as you can."

"Maybe so, but you'll probably be scared to death when we get to working on one of those steep roofs."

"Don't count on it."

Although the Davis boys grumbled, they had to admit the girls did as well as they did themselves. Neither Brenda nor her friend complained regardless of how hot it was on the steep roof or how tired they were when night came.

There were a few Indian kids their age, standing silently to one side, watching them work. The kids from Fairview tried to talk to them, but when they did, the Indians giggled shyly and refused to say anything. Sometimes they turned away. That bothered Doug and Del.

"I've never seen anything like it, have you, Del?"

"I thought the kids in Guatemala were shy, but they aren't even in it compared to this bunch."

"Do you suppose there's anything we can do to make friends with them while we're here?"

"I don't know, but it's going to take a lot of doing; that's for sure."

"We'll have to pray about it."

The following evening when Del and Doug Davis finished work, they saw several Indian and Inuit guys about their own age in a little cluster down by the creek.

"What do you suppose they're doing?"

Doug shrugged. "I don't have a clue. Why don't we go down and find out?"

"Good idea. Maybe we can get acquainted with them."

The Davis brothers sauntered down to the water's edge. "Hi," they called.

The boys looked up and grinned but did not speak.

"What're you doing?" Doug asked curiously.

"We're trying to get the ball." With that the speaker took the long stick from his companion and leaned forward in an effort to reach the volleyball resting on the sand near the water's edge.

"Here," Doug volunteered, "there's no need to make such a big deal out of it. I'll get it for you."

They stepped aside silently.

He moved forward with confidence and leaned out to reach the ball.

"Hey!" he cried, trying to lift one foot and then the other. He could not move! "Hey!" Terror honed his voice. "Hey! I'm sinking!"

Del Davis's eyes widened. While they stood there watching, his brother sank to his knees in the sand!

Again Doug tried to move, but a strange, invisible force tightened its grip on him.

"What's going on?" He struggled frantically to free himself; but the harder he fought, the faster he sank into the sand. The color fled from his cheeks, leaving them ashen.

Quicksand! No wonder the guys had been trying

to reach the ball with a pole. They knew about the treacherous loose sand, and they hadn't even warned him! Even now when they saw what was happening, they made no move to help. He stared back at the dark, grinning faces around him. What was worse, their eyes were laughing at him. His anger surged.

"Del!" he cried. "Don't just stand there! Do something!"

By this time Del was panic-stricken too. He would have gone out to his brother, but Doug stopped him with a shout of warning. "Don't! It'll grab you too!"

Del whirled. "Come on, you guys! Help me!"

The Inuit and Indian boys still did not move. Instead, they looked at one another, their grins continuing to broaden.

"Come on!" he pleaded. "Help me!"

# CHAPTER 7

# A FUNNY WAY TO MAKE FRIENDS

Doug's desperation crescendoed. "This isn't funny!" By this time, he realized that struggling only caused him to sink faster into the bottomless, jelly-like sand. Still, even though he remained motionless, he kept moving steadily downward.

Del grabbed the nearest Indian boy by the arm frantically. "We *can't* let him stay in there! We've got to do something, or he'll be in over his head and suffocate!"

The tallest boy said solemnly, "He'll get out some time. Maybe if he sinks deep enough, some Chinese guy will grab his feet and pull him out."

They all laughed at that, as though it was the funniest joke any of them had ever heard.

Del wrenched the pole from the hands of another boy and thrust it out. Doug clamped onto it with both hands like a drowning man might grasp a life preserver. Though Del pulled with all his strength, he could not stop his brother from sinking slowly into the shifting sand.

"What's the matter with you people?" Del almost screamed at them. "Get hold of this pole and help me!"

Still nobody moved.

"He can hold the pole up," an Inuit boy said calmly. "Then, when he sinks out of sight, at least people will know where he went."

Doug sank almost to his waist in the sand, and nothing he or Del did made any difference. He continued to settle deeper and deeper. Then, when the sand touched his belt, he stopped.

He looked at the boys in amazement, and his lower jaw sagged. "W-w-what happened?"

The laughter of the native boys rang out, echoing across the valley on the still air. They laughed so hard that tears filled their eyes and streamed down their cheeks. And still they couldn't stop.

Del and Doug grinned sheepishly. They didn't know what was going on, but whatever it was, the joke was on them.

"What's this all about?"

An Inuit boy who had been introduced to them earlier as Stoney Nicklie answered. "Your brother sank down to the permafrost. He won't go any farther."

With that he started to laugh again, and the others joined him.

"Man, you guys sure know how to scare a guy. I thought you were going to let that sand bury me."

When they stopped laughing, two of them hurried up to the toolshed for spades to dig Doug out. It was only a matter of a few minutes until they had moved enough of the sugar-fine sand to enable him to free himself. By the time he was safely on solid ground, he and Del were well acquainted with the other guys. There was John Nanalook, Wally Irwin, and Gust Aposik, besides Stoney Nicklie.

For some reason, the incident broke the barriers between them. They talked with their new friends until the dinner bell sounded.

"We've got to get going or we won't get anything to eat," Doug said. "We'll see you guys tomorrow after work."

Stoney Nicklie's eyes gleamed. "Do you want to come back and try our sand again?"

"No, thanks." He spoke with feeling. "I'll leave that for the next greenhorn if it's all right with you."

The Davis brothers walked back up to the house together.

"I was never so scared in all my life. I thought I was a goner, for sure," Doug remarked.

"So did I. And the way they stood around laughing made me so mad I could've clobbered them."

Doug laughed. "Me, too. When you get right down to it, I guess they're not much different than we are. We'd have done the same thing to one of them if they'd been visiting us and something like this happened."

When they were almost to the house, Doug stopped. "What do you say we keep this a little secret from the rest of the kids, okay?"

Del's face crinkled with merriment. "You mean, you don't want them to know what terrible danger you were in a little while ago?"

"That's the general idea."

"We'll see." He was still laughing when they went in to join the others.

The following afternoon, Stoney and Gus stopped by to watch Del and Doug work for a while. "Why are you doing that?" Stoney asked curiously.

Del didn't understand him. "The old roof leaked, so Bob asked us to put on a new one."

"Then you're being paid for it?"

"Oh, no, we're working for nothing."

His answer was bewildering to the Inuit lad. "You work for free? But why? It is not *your* roof. Why should you care if it leaks? Why do you come all the way from your home to fix a roof?"

Momentarily Del laid his hammer aside, searching for words to explain to Stoney the reason for their coming. "We came to help fix up the building here at the mission, so the missionaries won't have to do it themselves."

"Why? If it is nothing to you, why do you do it?"

"We want to help with some of the work, so they'll

have more time to talk to you and your family and friends about Jesus Christ."

Stoney Nicklie thought about that. Del could see by the perplexed look in his eyes that Stoney still did not understand what he was trying to tell him, but he didn't know what else to say. It must be hard for these people to accept the fact that the missionaries came with no ulterior motives. So many of the white people who came to live among them were there for selfish purposes.

On Saturday, Del and Doug saw the Inuit boys again. This time they acted as if they wanted to talk, and the Davis brothers took time to joke with them for a few minutes. Before they left, Del invited them to the church services the next day. They hesitated, as though they weren't sure whether they wanted to come.

"Are you going to be there?" Gust wanted to know.

"Oh, sure, I'll be there. And so will Doug; that is, unless he gets caught in the quicksand again. If he does, I think we'll leave him there."

The next morning, a few moments before the service was to begin, the door opened, and Stoney and Gust and their friends filed in. They shuffled into the chapel self-consciously and stood by the door until Del and Doug saw them and hurried back to greet them.

"It's sure good to see you," Doug said.

Bob and Patti Kline were only a few steps behind

them. "We're glad you guys came to church this morning," Bob said, extending a huge, friendly hand.

A thin smile lit Stoney's dark face. "Our friends asked us."

After the service, when everyone else had gone, Bob sought out the Davis brothers. "I've got to know something. How did you guys get next to Stoney and his pals?"

"We started talking to them, and finally, yesterday, we asked them to come to church," Del answered. "Why?"

"I've been working on them for a couple of years, but this is the first time they would ever come to a service. I can't figure it out."

Then Del told him about the ball in the creek and how everyone had laughed at Doug when he got caught in the quicksand. "That's the only thing that happened, though, and there's sure nothing in that to make anyone want to start going to church."

Bob was still bewildered. He had been praying that the kids from Fairview would be a blessing while they were at the station and that their testimony would make an impression on the guys and girls their own age, but he hadn't expected to see the results of that testimony so quickly.

"I suppose they saw that you have a sense of humor too," he said, "and they were attracted by it – that and the fact that you didn't get mad."

"I was *plenty* mad for a while," Doug told him,

"until I found out I wasn't going to sink to China in that stuff."

"You were able to laugh at yourself. That's one thing that goes far with the people here." The missionary took a deep breath. "I guess that shows we never know what the Lord is going to use to help break down the barriers. You've already been able to do more than I've been able to do with Stoney and his pals."

Doug and Del grinned their pleasure. That made it all worthwhile. In the days that followed, they prayed more fervently than ever for their new Inuit and Indian friends.

The first two days of the following week, Del and Doug didn't see their new friends at all, and they began to wonder if something had happened to hurt their feelings. When they did come around again, however, it was to offer their services with the roofing. By this time Brenda and her friend had been put on another job, and the Davis boys were working alone. John Nanalook came forward and spoke for all of them.

"We don't have anything to do today," he said. "Maybe we can help you." His shyness took over suddenly. His voice lowered, and embarrassment stained his dark cheeks. "That is, if you need help."

Doug spoke up at once. "Sure thing. The more who work, the quicker we'll get done."

They were just getting up on the roof when Bob

Kline stopped by. He thanked the young guys for their offer of help and suggested splitting the group. He had Del stay on the roof with John and Wally to finish there. Doug, he sent over to the infirmary with Stoney and Gust Aposik. They were going to put a new roof on that building too.

"That's great," Doug said quickly. "Come on, guys. We'll show those other guys how to put a roof on."

Del and his companions laughed at the challenge and set to work furiously.

Working with the Indian boys, Del and Doug became better acquainted with them than they had ever thought possible. They discovered that the Inuit and Indians were not stoic and unemotional as they had been taught. They laughed and joked and talked as much as anyone. They were always shy and quiet around strangers, however. They had been taught that it was impolite to be bold and talkative around those they did not know.

At first, Del and Doug only got to know the four guys who came to help them, but as the days passed, others began to come around. They watched curiously, but it wasn't long until they began to volunteer their services. Before the week was out, more than half a dozen Indian and Inuit boys could be found working on the buildings. At the same time, attendance among the guys at Sunday services picked up. Stoney and his friends were always there, and some of the others began to attend some of the meetings.

At the midweek staff prayer meeting, which the volunteers from Fairview attended with the missionaries, Bob thanked the Lord for this new development among the boys and challenged the girls to find some girls their age to add to the group.

"When you kids first decided to come here, I must be frank and tell you that I didn't see this particular area of service. I thought solely of the work you should be doing. This, however, is very exciting."

His voice crescendoed as he talked about what was taking place. "You have a rapport with the kids that those of us who are older don't have. I have a feeling that when we look back on this summer, we will remember your visit most for the way in which you've helped to break down the barriers of the high-school age guys and girls against the services and the gospel."

He went on to tell them that they had never had any strong Christian young people at this particular mission station, either white or Indian, and that the kids had never before seen a teenager who walked with Christ.

"This is the thing that is making the impact right now," he continued. "Stoney and the others are seeing guys their own age, whom they like and respect, who also walk with Christ. It has to have an effect on them."

He paused and turned to the girls. "I know the Lord has given the guys this chance to work with the boys their age, so we can't give them credit for it, except to thank God that they were willing and ready to make friends and to use that friendship to get the guys to start coming to our services. I'd like to covenant with you girls to pray that God will provide you the same chance while you're here."

As he continued talking, Brenda, Sandy, and DeeDee nodded solemnly in agreement. Already in their hearts they were asking God to help them make friends with the Indian and Inuit girls and to be a witness to them for Christ.

# CHAPTER 8

# CONFRONTATION

The flaming early morning sun seemed to fill the cloudless sky and reflected off the water with a dazzling beauty that hurt the eyes. Usually she was sensitive to such things, but that morning Marty Ross was scarcely aware that she was squinting against the brilliance of the day as she faced the hostility of her companions just outside their motel in Anchorage, Alaska.

"Susan and I were talking about it again last night," Karla said petulantly. "You've been absolutely impossible ever since you talked with that high-school kid about religion. You won't do anything anymore. If we'd known the trip was going to turn out like this, we wouldn't have come."

Before she could answer, Susan spoke up. "To be honest with you, you're the last one we would ever have guessed would flip out over religion. It wouldn't really matter, except that this is your car. So, if you don't feel like going someplace, we're stranded."

Marty chewed her nails. How could she tell her friends what had happened in her life that would cause her to give up going to night clubs and even to quit smoking? How could she tell them what it meant to walk with Jesus Christ when she knew so little about it herself? There were no words to say what she felt without sounding silly to Karla and Susan.

This was one thing she hadn't expected when she confessed her sin and gave her heart and life to Jesus Christ. Brenda and the others on the church bus had found it so easy to tell what Jesus Christ meant to them. She expected to have the same freedom. When she didn't, it was bewildering.

"It wouldn't have hurt you to go in with those guys and have a drink," Karla persisted. "After all, it wasn't as if we were pickups. We knew Paul's sister from school, and he and his friends had been counting on taking us out to show us the town. We'd have had a great time today if it hadn't been for you. You had to spoil everything."

Maybe it would have been all right to go along with them and order a coke instead of liquor. Marty wasn't sure now that she'd done the right thing. Maybe it would be fun just to go out with some guys for a few laughs for a change. She still wasn't sure.

Marty took the car keys from her purse and held

them nervously. "I'm sorry." She wasn't sorry for what she had done but for ruining the day for her friends.

"Oh sure. It's a little late for regrets," Karla snapped.

"What's wrong with not drinking?" Marty asked. "Besides, when Paul offered to take us just to dinner, you two wouldn't go," she said defensively.

"He didn't mean it," Susan replied.

Marty shrugged. "I've already told you that I'm sorry I spoiled your good time. What more can I do?"

"You can forget about going out to that mission station or whatever you call it," Karla said, her bitterness growing. "You could at least forget about going to see that bunch of religious fanatics. It's going to be a terrible drag for Susan and me."

Marty knew it would be easier for her to give in to them than to insist that they go with her out to the place where Brenda and her friends were staying, but she had been intrigued by the mission and she would never get another chance to see it.

"It won't take us long," she countered. "I won't ask you to stay there more than an hour with me."

Susan spoke up. "What you mean is that you want to get us over there so *they* can work on us. You want to convert *us* before we go back."

Marty did not answer her accusation. "You heard what the girl at the visitor center said. The drive over there is beautiful."

"I can just imagine."

"Why don't we go and have breakfast?" Marty suggested. "We can talk about it there."

"There's nothing more to talk about."

They were just pulling out of the motel drive when a car braked to a stop nearby, horn honking.

Karla's eyes brightened. "There's Paul!" She leaned forward and waved at the youthful driver, who had careened into the driveway and was getting out of his car.

Marty stopped, as he came striding over to them.

"Say now, I guess I am in luck," he exclaimed. "A couple of minutes more and I'd have missed you. That would've been tragic."

Karla was the one who answered him, breathlessly. "We're going out for breakfast, Paul. Why don't you join us?"

He looked at Marty, a question in his eyes. "That's why I came by," he said to her. "I was going to ask *you* to join *me*."

Marty knew he was asking her to go with him alone, but she couldn't do that. Not now, anyway. Karla was already so angry with her she couldn't speak civilly. If she went off with Paul, the rest of the trip would be ruined. Besides, she didn't care to go with him. He was all right, but she preferred the trip to the mission station.

"Then everything is working out fine," Karla said aloud.

He glanced at Karla, who was sitting in the backseat

alone, and then at Marty. "I think I'd better drive my own car," he said. "You go where you were going, and I'll follow you."

Karla's face clouded, and she settled back into the seat in silence. That was about what she could expect from Marty, she decided, fuming inwardly. She'd made such a thing of not going in with the others for a cocktail. Now she was trying to steal Paul. That religion of hers was just an act. What else could it be? Before leaving on this trip, Marty had been able to drink them all under the table and usually did, every chance she had. She couldn't have changed all that fast. It had to be put on. She had made a show in front of Brenda what-ever-her-name-was and the rest of those religious fanatics, and last night she had put on an act to impress Paul.

Karla frowned.

She tried to maneuver so she could sit next to Paul when they got into the café, but he sat at the opposite end, where he was the nearest to Marty. Karla broke in from time to time with questions designed to let him know she was still in the group. He answered as courteously as possible but quickly directed his attention to Marty again.

"By some wonderful coincidence, I didn't have to work today," he said. "So I decided to come over and see if I could give you a personal, guided tour of our beautiful Alaska."

"You're a knight in shining armor," Karla broke

in. "Marty has been trying to tell us that we ought to go someplace east of Palmer."

"That's an excellent choice," he said. "You couldn't go to a more magnificent spot anywhere in our state." He turned to Marty once more. "I want to commend you on your excellent judgment. I will show you things so breathtaking, they will hurt your eyes."

She smiled graciously. "Thank you, Paul, but I'm afraid you don't understand. You see, there's a specific place I want to go."

"So?" He shrugged as though that was a small matter. "We'll go anywhere your pretty little heart wants to go."

"Please, let me finish."

His smile fled. "Sure," he retorted testily, "go right ahead. Don't mind me. I'm just trying to be agreeable."

"I'm sorry." She didn't know why everything had to be so difficult that day. All she wanted to do was to make it clear to him that she wasn't insisting on the drive to Palmer because of the beauty of the area. "I've been wanting to go to a mission station east of there," she said quietly, "to see the work they're doing. A very good friend of mine is there and–" Her voice trailed off in the face of his belligerence.

"You really are on a religious kick, aren't you?"

Marty blushed.

"When you were giving us that 'I'm too good to drink' bit last night, I thought you were putting us on." He leaned forward, eyelids narrowing. "You actually mean all of that, don't you? It's for real."

"I don't know for sure what you're talking about." Marty was furious at herself for being on the defensive. "I don't drink anymore, and I have given my life to Jesus Christ. Christ has somehow made me see things differently. Drinking doesn't even appeal to me. I think I've found the answer to a lot of whys I've had, and Christ can mean the same thing to you, Paul, to anyone."

He stared at her. The admiration left his eyes. "I don't think I'd feel very comfortable going with anyone who's so weird," he said scornfully. "I'd be afraid that I'd cause you to lose a little of your holiness by associating with me, and I wouldn't want to do that." He pushed back from the table, not waiting to order. "Pardon me for wasting your time."

He was about to get to his feet when Karla caught his eye. "*Maybe* you've been looking at the wrong one of us," she said, smiling.

"That's quite obvious."

She smiled coyly. "Don't judge all three of us by our little Sunday school girl. She was okay when we left home, but some religious kook got hold of her. This is the way she turned out."

The anger left his face. "Maybe today isn't going to be such a waste after all. And just what did you have in mind?"

She flashed a triumphant, knowing look at Marty.

She'd shown her this time! *Now* let her bite her nails and wish she hadn't been so pious! "I thought you could show Susan and me the sights around Anchorage, while Marty runs off to the mountains to pray."

His laughter was brittle. "I've got a better idea. Why don't you let Susan go with the little missionary to pray, and I'll show *you* the sights of Anchorage."

Triumphantly Karla pushed back from the table and stood. "That sounds great. I'll see you girls tonight at the motel."

Paul corrected her. "Late tonight – or should I say early tomorrow morning?"

With that, they were gone, and Susan and Marty were alone. After a while, Marty reached out and touched the other girl's arm with her hand. "I'm sorry you're stuck with me today, Susan."

"I know Karla as well as you do. She saw a man, and when that happens, she flips out. It was nothing you did."

When they finished eating breakfast and were drinking a second cup of coffee, Marty went back to their plans for the day.

"I'm sorry I've been so selfish in insisting that we go out to the mission station," she said. "We'll forget about that and do anything you want to do."

"Oh, no," Susan said quickly. "I really would like to go out there with you. I think it would be very interesting."

Marty's smile was warm. "That makes me feel better."

Susan was more good-natured than Karla, so she was more willing to accept Marty's new lifestyle. Marty knew, though, that Susan's willingness did not indicate any change in her own thinking.

A mile slipped by before Susan said anything more. "Tell me," she began, "were we as rude and as ungracious to you last night as Paul and Karla were just now?"

The embarrassment of the night before was still enough to bring the flame back to Marty's cheeks. That had probably been the most difficult few minutes she had put in since the night she asked Christ into her life.

"Why don't we talk about something else, okay?" Marty asked, not looking at the girl next to her.

"Sure," Susan answered.

# CHAPTER 9

## SANDY'S DILEMMA

**S**andy Cole received a letter from her mother in Los Angeles, a long, rambling account of trips to exclusive little dress shops and expensive restaurants and, of course, Disneyland.

"I know you're having a good time, Sandy, but I can't help wishing you were here. We would have so much fun doing the shops together. I've seen so many darling little dresses I'd like to have bought for you if you were only with me so I could see how you like them."

The girl paused. She didn't know why, but her mother's chattering about shopping and new clothes bothered her. It had caused her dad so much trouble, for one thing. Her mother kept spending and spending and spending, even when his business was almost bankrupt. Buying new clothes and going places seemed to be Mom's answer for everything. Whenever Sandy wanted to do something she didn't approve of, she tried to bribe her with new clothes or a trip.

The girl directed her attention back to the letter. As she suspected, her mother wasn't long in warning her against her dad.

"I hope you aren't believing everything he tells you these days. I know him better than anyone else, Sandy. He'll promise you anything and make you believe he's going to do anything in order to get his way. He wants to get you away from me, and he's not going to be satisfied until he does. That was the real reason I didn't want you to make that trip to Alaska. I'm sorry now that I let Robert talk me into giving you permission to go."

Tears filled Sandy's eyes. She didn't know why her mother always had to believe the worst about Dad. It didn't make any difference how hard he tried to do things right, she would never believe he wasn't scheming to box her into a corner or to get an unfair advantage over her. He certainly hadn't given her any reason to feel that way either since he had become a Christian. Still, she refused to believe that he had changed.

Sandy left the building and walked down by the creek alone. During the last few days, she had been giving more thought than ever to moving in with her dad. The same reasons came into her mind as when she had thought it all out before. If she lived with him, he could help her to live closer to God. He would always be there when she needed to talk with someone about God's will for her life.

Let her mother have Robert Fenwick if that was who she wanted. They would probably be glad to have Sandy move, so they wouldn't have to bother with her. Robert practically said he felt that way the night she overheard them talking about their trip to Los Angeles.

Well, he wouldn't have to worry about her anymore. By the time school started, she would be living in her dad's apartment. That would make it better for everybody. She and Dad would have a home of their own, and they'd both be happier than either of them had been since the divorce.

It wasn't going to be easy to get her dad to agree to her moving in with him. She didn't know why he was so stubborn about such things. He really wanted it, too; she was sure of that, but he would give her plenty of resistance. He'd talk about what the court said when the divorce was granted and how she had been placed in her mother's custody. She knew all of that was true, but she couldn't see that it meant anything now. She was old enough to know where she wanted to live.

Sandy turned, once she made up her mind about moving in with her father, and started to look for him. She finally located him in the school building, where he was working.

"Dad," she said, scarcely above a whisper, "I've got something important to talk to you about."

He noted the time. "Honey, can it wait? We have an awful lot of work to finish this afternoon."

Her lower lip trembled, and, for an instant, she was afraid she would start to cry. "I suppose it can, but I got a letter from Mom, and I want to talk to you about it."

She knew that would bring him. He left what he was doing, and, taking her by the arm, guided her outside, where they could speak privately.

"What is it, Sandy? What's wrong?"

"I got this long letter from Mom this afternoon," she began, "and it made me see that I've got to talk to you about something real important."

She didn't know why it should be so hard to approach him about moving into his apartment and keeping house for him. She was sure he wanted her to live with him as badly as she did, even though he had never said much about it.

"Is your mother all right?"

"She's fine." Sandy pulled herself erect. "I've just decided that I want to move in with you when we get home."

"You can't mean that, Sandy."

"But I do," she said desperately. "It's not going to do you any good to try to talk me out of it. I've gone over it and over it in my mind. I know what I want." All the things she had been thinking rushed out. She told him how her mom kept after her every time she was with her dad, how hard it was to live a Christian life when she got no help at home, and how it hurt to see Robert Fenwick and her mother living together.

"I can understand all of those things," he said, "but the judge–"

"I don't care what the judge says. I know what I *want.*" Tears came to her eyes, but she was so distraught she made no attempt to wipe them away. "It would be so wonderful if you and I were together. We could have Bible study together, just the two of us, and I could cook and clean and wash for you. You wouldn't have to be by yourself anymore."

Brad eyed his daughter narrowly. This was something he hadn't expected. He had been careful not to say anything to Sandy about her mother and had tried to get her to treat Robert Fenwick respectfully. There were times, however, when it had been difficult for him to accept the situation, and he would rather have had Sandy with him. Yes, he had to admit that Sandy's proposal was tempting. He was so very lonely, and she would be able to help him. He never had been the sort to do much cooking and cleaning. If he had to take care of things alone, the place would be an awful mess. Right now he had a woman who came in a couple of times a week to clean it up for him.

"But the court placed you in your mother's custody," he protested.

"I know that, but I'm going to be a junior in high school next year. What I want ought to count for something." She grasped his arm with trembling fingers.

He looked away momentarily. Now that Brad thought about it, he could remember hearing about a number of cases where a judge allowed an older child to make the decision as to which parent he wanted to live with. At the time of the divorce, he could not have expected anything else with the sort of record he had. Now, however, he had established himself as a sober, upright citizen. There would be a good chance of Sandy's getting court permission to come and live with him. He had to admit the idea was appealing. He missed Gladys, but he was sure he missed Sandy even more.

"Let's pray about it," he suggested.

She frowned her disapproval. "I already know what I want to do."

"Don't you think it would be better for us to ask God what He would have us do?"

"I guess so," she agreed reluctantly," but I've been thinking about it a long time, and when I got that letter this afternoon, I realized that I simply *can't* stay with Mother and Robert any longer."

They agreed to pray often. Then Brad said, "Before we get home, we'll decide whether we ought to try it, okay?"

"You will let me have a say, won't you?"

"Of course, I will."

Sandy went back to her job, a new exhilaration taking hold of her. She would be moving in with her dad as soon as he could work out the details, she decided, and that was going to be wonderful. She was so excited about it, she began to wish she was home now so she could begin keeping house for him.

The following morning, Marty and Susan drove into the mission station. DeeDee and Sandy saw the car and ran out to meet them.

"Hi there," DeeDee exclaimed.

Marty looked around for the girl who had led her to Christ while she said, "I just had to come out to see the station before we go back home, and Susan was good enough to come along."

"I figured I'd come and see how the other half lives," Susan said lightly.

By this time Brenda had joined them. For several minutes everybody was laughing and talking at the same time as they went over the things they had done since seeing each other.

At last Marty grew serious. "We really came out to see what goes on at a mission station. Aren't you going to show us around before it gets dark?"

Brenda checked her watch. "Great! We'll have thirteen hours, at least."

"Good," Marty answered. "I want to see every-thing." Excitement gleamed in her eyes. "I'm anxious to see how the regular residents around here live and what the missionaries are doing." She paused, remembering her companion. "How about you, Susan? What would you like to see?"

Susan's cheeks colored slightly. "I've got something else in mind."

"Like what?" DeeDee asked.

"I'm anxious to see what kind of oddballs would be willing to come to a place like this just to change people's religion."

Embarrassment darkened Marty's features. She hoped Brenda and her friends wouldn't take offense at Susan's bluntness.

"It–it isn't a matter of trying to change anybody's religion," DeeDee said. "It's more than that, a lot more. Following Jesus Christ is a way of life. That's why the missionaries are here. They want to present Jesus Christ to the people who haven't confessed their sin and put their trust in Him. They want to give them a chance to become Christians."

Susan stared questioningly at DeeDee, but she was still derisive. "It might *seem* like something else to you, but as far as I'm concerned, it's the same difference."

Brenda changed the subject quickly. "Well, if we're going to look around, we'd better get with it."

The girls got into the car and directed Marty to the nearest village. As they visited among the villagers, they watched for an opportunity to talk further with Susan about her own need of Jesus Christ. They wanted to tell her more of what He had done for them and what He could do for her, but there was no opportunity.

Susan sensed the fact that they wanted to talk with her about Christ and was determined to keep them from doing so. Although the girls tried hard to get back to the subject, she controlled the conversation.

Sandy couldn't help thinking how much Susan's actions reminded her of her own mother. Gladys Fenwick ducked the gospel whenever she could. If Sandy brought up the subject, her mother had something she had to do immediately. She would get out the vacuum cleaner and run it noisily until her daughter gave up and went to her room, or she would decide she had to go shopping, or run to the library, or call someone about a committee meeting.

It was so difficult to try to reach a person like Marty's friend or her own mother. Susan's determination to avoid hearing about Jesus Christ had a disquieting effect on Sandy that, for some reason, dampened her elation about the possibility of moving in with her dad.

At last the time came for Marty and Susan to leave. The girls walked to the car with them. "I wish you didn't have to go now," Brenda said. "It's almost time for dinner."

Marty hesitated. It was obvious that she didn't want to go so soon. "What do you think, Susan?"

Before the other girl could say anything, DeeDee

broke in. "What's more, we're having a service tonight, and Brenda is going to speak."

"What about?"

DeeDee answered, "Why don't you stay and find out?"

Marty glanced at her companion.

"If you're going back early on my account, forget it," Susan said. "Karla's got her hooks in the only man we've met who's looked interesting to me, and she probably won't be in until one or two o'clock. There's no reason for us to get back early."

A large group of villagers came to the service that evening, filing into the chapel, and taking seats at the back. They sang a few hymns and choruses, Danny read the Scripture and led in prayer, and Bob asked those who were to give their testimonies to come to the platform.

Brenda was the last to speak. She stood to her feet nervously when she was introduced and approached the podium.

She told the group very graphically what her life had been like back in high school the year before and what it was like now that she had asked Jesus Christ to give her a new life. At that point Susan, who was squirming miserably, stood up, pushed by the other girls, and stormed out of the building. Brenda stared at her. She forgot what she was saying and stumbled for words miserably.

Bob Kline closed the meeting with prayer. As

soon as it was over, several came forward to talk to Brenda. DeeDee and Sandy were among the first. "We're all so proud of you! You were terrific!" they assured her.

Brenda scarcely heard them. The hurt gleamed in her eyes, and her voice trembled as if she was about to cry. "What happened to Susan? Is she ill?"

Marty came up in time to hear the younger girl's question. "I haven't the faintest idea, but I don't think so."

Brenda's gaze wandered over the chapel, as though she half expected to see Susan standing in the back.

"I'm sorry if I offended her."

"You needn't be. That talk was wonderful. If there was anything wrong, it was with Susan."

After a time, the crowd thinned, and the girls walked with Marty out to her car. Susan was scrunched in the corner of the front seat, sitting so low they could only see the top of her head.

"I guess the service tonight was a little too strong for her and especially that talk of yours, Brenda," Marty said softly.

The other girl drew a deep breath. "Would it do any good if I went over and apologized to her?"

Marty shook her head. "Maybe you were supposed to hit her hard by telling what Christ has done in your life. Let's not spoil it."

At that moment, as though on signal, Susan put

down the car window. "What are you going to do," she demanded irritably, "stand there and talk all night?"

"I'm sorry," Marty said. "I'm ready to go now."

"It's about time."

The little group stood in comparative silence until Marty backed around and drove out the narrow lane to the graveled road that led back to town.

"I didn't expect to ever see her again," Brenda said.

"Neither did we," DeeDee added.

Sandy walked back to the house alone, the ache in her heart growing. What Susan did was so like her mother that she was almost overwhelmed. It seemed that she had been praying for her mother as long as she could remember and there wasn't any change. Would she *ever* give her life to Christ?

# CHAPTER 10

# SCOTTY'S CABIN

**M**issionary Bob Kline stepped back to survey the big school building Doug and Del and their Alaskan friends had been helping on, a smile crinkling his bronzed face.

"That's looking great!" he exclaimed. "Simply great. Another day or two and everything around here ought to be finished in good shape. Now, what do you think of that?"

Del grinned back at him. "I'm disappointed that you can't find anything else for us to do."

"Has it been as bad as all that?"

"Oh, no," Doug said quickly. "It's been fun working with you this summer. I wouldn't trade this experience for anything else we might have done."

"It's been a tremendous experience for us too." Bob glanced over at Stoney and Gust and John, who were standing nearby. "I'm sure we wouldn't have gotten half the work done this summer if your youth group hadn't come. There've been some other gains, too, that we can't measure by the same yardstick." Although he didn't say so, both Del and Doug knew he was thinking about the change in the attitude of the Indian and Inuit boys.

"I'm glad all the work is done before we have to go back home," Del said.

Gust Aposik came sauntering over to where they were standing. "Why don't you stay with us?"

"We'd like to, but we have to go back to Fairview to go to school."

"You can go to school here."

John Nanalook and Stoney nodded in agreement. "There are lots of things you could do around the mission, isn't that right, Mr. Kline?"

"It certainly is. Maybe Del and Doug can come back again next year."

By midafternoon the following day, the boys finished work on the building and suggested to Bob that he find something else for them to do until the first of the week, when the bus was to leave for Minnesota.

"I want you guys to go out with the friends you've made here and enjoy yourselves," he said. "There's going to be no more work for you here this summer."

Stoney and the others were waiting for them. They all walked down to the fast-moving stream together, talking about the fact that Del and Doug would soon be heading South.

"There are so many things we wanted to do while you were here," Gust said, "but we didn't get to do any of them. We didn't even get to take you up to the old gold mine." Disappointment edged his voice.

The Davis boys were both sorry they hadn't had the chance to go up to the abandoned gold mine a dozen miles up the river. That was one place they had wanted to see ever since they heard about it.

"Maybe we could go up there tomorrow and spend the night," Doug suggested.

The Inuit boys eyed each other uneasily.

"Nobody would care if we spent the night there, would they?"

There was a brief hesitation, and Doug repeated his question.

"Nobody except old Scotty."

"And who's old Scotty?" Del asked.

John Nanalook laughed, a bit nervously, it seemed to Doug and Del. "That's just a little joke of ours. There isn't any 'old Scotty.' At least there isn't any old Scotty *now*. Nobody'll care if we spend the night at the gold mine."

That settled the matter. Before the Alaskan boys left the mission that afternoon, it was decided that the five of them would go up to the mining camp the following day and come back the next.

"Good," Doug added. "Maybe we can even find some gold."

Gust grinned. "Everybody who goes there thinks

maybe he'll find a nugget as big as his head, but nobody has ever found anything there that I know of, in a long time, anyway. Don't plan on getting rich tomorrow. Okay?"

* * *

Sandy and her friends had also finished work and were packing their things for the trip home the first of the next week. Ever since Susan had visited the mission, Sandy had been disturbed. She tried hard not to show it, but Danny and Kay noticed and sought her out.

"Is there something wrong, Sandy?" Danny asked, keeping his voice down so they would not be overheard.

"Not exactly." She laughed nervously. "I mean there's nothing wrong with *me*. I'm fine."

"I heard you got a letter from home yesterday," Kay said gently. "Is everything all right there?"

Sandy had difficulty raising her gaze to meet Kay's. "I guess I'm upset about Mom."

Once she started, it was easier for her to talk. She went on to explain how she had been praying for her mother and Robert Fenwick for so very long and had tried to talk to them so many times, but they wouldn't listen.

"I've finally reached the place where I'm afraid they're *never* going to give themselves to Christ."

"I can see why you would feel that way," Danny told her, "but God is able to save us *and* our families, and He will. There are times when it's hard for us to realize that, because He doesn't work on the same timetable that we do."

As he continued to talk, her assurance came slowly back, and before he finished, she was smiling again.

"You have no idea how good that makes me feel, Danny. I'd given up hope."

"We should never do that. You have one big advantage over a lot of people with loved ones who aren't Christians. You live in the same house with your mother and Robert. If you keep on praying, God might give *you* the opportunity to lead them to Christ."

Sandy flinched. She wouldn't be living with her mother and Robert very long after she got back home. How would she be able to influence them for Christ after she moved out? And what would her mother think of her Savior if Sandy did turn her back on her? Suddenly Sandy felt weak and sick inside.

* * *

The following morning, Del and Doug got up even earlier than usual. As they looked out, a cold mist was specking the window and the wind was swirling down the little valley from the mountains. Even from the inside where it was warm, they could see that the temperature had dropped considerably.

Doug groaned aloud. "Today we were supposed to go up to the old mine. Do you suppose we'll be able to go?" His disappointment was evident.

"If we don't," Del said, "we won't be able to get up there at all."

"It's sure not going to be much fun hiking up there in stuff like this and camping out."

The Inuit boys came while Del and Doug were having breakfast. The Davis boys didn't see them, but when they came out of the staff dining hall after breakfast, they were waiting, hunkered against the cold, wet wind.

"So, you guys did show up," Doug said.

"Are you ready?" Stoney Nicklie asked.

"Do you mean you still want to go?"

"We do if you do."

"Now you didn't think we'd be too soft to make a trip up to the mine just because of a little rain, did you?"

John Nanalook shrugged. "Who knows how soft you are?"

Del looked around, ignoring the fine mist that rode on the driving wind. He didn't know why it made so much difference to him, but he couldn't have their Inuit friends thinking the weather could keep them from doing something they planned on.

"Why don't we wait an hour and see if it lets up. Okay?" Doug suggested.

They went into Del and Doug's room and waited half the morning. The wind and rain still gave no sign of stopping.

After a long while, Gust Aposik stood and went to the door. "Do we go or don't we?" he asked.

The Davis boys glanced at each other. "If you guys are game, so are we."

They slung their gear over their shoulders and trudged alongside the turbulent creek. "How long do you think it'll take us to get up to the mining camp?"

Gust Aposik grinned. "We aren't much more than away from the mission and already you are wondering how long it takes us to get there. What's the matter? Are you getting tired already, or is the wind and the rain too much for you?"

"I was just concerned about you, Gust," Doug said, laughing.

"Don't you worry about me."

They walked on in silence. Del knew that as far as the other villagers and themselves were concerned, Gust and his friends were men. They were expected to go out on the hunt with the others and walk long miles stalking their prey. At times there was little for them to eat. It would take more than a little rain and wind and cold to cause any of them to turn back. That was all the more reason why the Davis boys had to keep plugging along, regardless of how cold and miserable the journey was. They couldn't have their friends turning back because of them.

For half an hour, they made their way along the creek, clenching their teeth against the bite of the wind and the rain. Suddenly Doug laughed. Del turned toward him. "What's the matter with you?"

"I was just thinking how stupid we are, coming out on a hike like this in the wet and cold, when we could be sitting in a nice warm house."

"It's trips like this that make you appreciate those nice warm houses."

They plodded steadily on in spite of the cold and the wet. They were hungry at noon, but the Inuit boys said nothing about eating, so Doug and Del didn't mention it. It would have been miserable stopping to eat, anyway.

Although the boys tried to keep up the pace they set for themselves on leaving the mission station, it was inevitable that the weather would slow them. They expected to be at the gold mine in a couple of hours, but most of the afternoon had been trudged away before they finally reached it.

It was nothing like they thought it would be. Actually, it was not much different than the Indian villages they had visited, although it was small and uninhabited. The buildings were in a terrible state of disrepair. Most of the windows had long since been knocked out. Doors sagged on their hinges, and roofs leaked. Doug could not keep from expressing himself. "Boy, this sure isn't much," he said.

His brother eyed him critically. "What did you expect, the Hilton?"

Gust Aposik told them the history of the place, how the first white man to come into the area had discovered gold there and caused a real rush that lasted three years before the gold and the faith in it were gone.

"A long time ago, many men lived here," he concluded.

Del nodded in agreement. Bob Kline had already told him and Doug much of the story. He told them about that first prospector, a half crazed Scot who claimed to have struck it rich. He tried to keep his find a secret, but the news leaked out, and there was a great rush into the area. The poor man who made the discovery was killed before he was able to prove his claim.

"I suppose you know all about old Scotty McRoberts, don't you?" Del asked matter-of-factly.

Stoney Nicklie's eyes widened. *"Everybody* around here knows about Scotty." There was a strange hush to Stoney's voice. "They say he still walks the mountains looking for the man who stole his claim!"

Gust shivered. "Don't talk about such things! We have to stay here tonight."

Del was about to tease them about the old Scot who was supposed to haunt the area, but the fear in their eyes stopped him.

"Well," he changed the subject abruptly, "we'd better find a building that's dry enough to spread these sleeping bags out in."

John Nanalook frowned. "You–you mean we're going to sleep inside?" His voice quavered in spite of his efforts to control it.

"I can tell you one thing; we're not going to sleep *outside* on a night like this. Not as long as there are some buildings around that will keep a little of the rain off of us."

There was a long, taut hush. At last Del turned to John. "It's all right if we go inside and spread out our sleeping bags, isn't it?"

There was another moment or two of silence as the Davis boys looked from one fearful Inuit face to the other.

"Maybe we ought to go back to the mission," Doug suggested. "We ought to be able to make it by midnight."

Stoney did not agree. "No, we'll stay here. It's okay to go inside and stay."

The boys peered into several abandoned buildings before choosing one that seemed to offer the most protection from the rain and wind.

"How does this look to you?"

John answered, "It is all right, except that this was Scotty's cabin!"

# CHAPTER 11

# A SCARY NIGHT AND SAD FAREWELLS

The Inuit boys stared mutely at their white friends, concern gleaming in their dark eyes. Their somber faces took on a strange, ashen look, and they shifted from one foot to the other. Indecision marked every move they made.

At last John Nanalook spoke, making an effort to sound casual and undisturbed. "There're some better places farther upriver. How about looking at them before we decide to stay here?"

There was a sudden surge of wind, and the rain increased, pelting the boys with savage intensity. Del seemed to be swayed by the argument, but Doug shook his head with finality.

"Nothing doing! You guys can tramp around in the cold and rain for another hour if you want to, but that's not for me. This building looks dry enough, and there's a stove in there, so we can build a little fire and warm up. I don't think we can find anything else half as good, and I'm not about to look anymore."

"It's dry in here, and we can build a fire. I don't think we can find anything better than that," Del said.

"Neither do I. Let's see how quickly we can get the stove working," Doug said with finality.

John Nanalook acted as though he really wanted to protest, but couldn't quite bring himself to do so. Appealingly, he turned to Gust Aposik, hoping to prod his friend into voicing objection. "What do you think, Gust? You've been here before. Can we find a better place to stay?"

But Del, like his brother, didn't want to go any farther. "I vote for staying right here."

"But there's Scotty!" Stoney exclaimed. "They say he was killed in a storm like this, maybe in this very same house. They say he is seen roaming the buildings every night it storms!"

Del did not realize the depth of their disturbance. "I hope he takes his shoes off before he comes tramping around in here. I don't want to be woke up."

"Don't talk that way!" John whispered tautly.

Doug changed the subject. "Let's forget about old Scotty, or none of us will sleep tonight."

Although the Inuit boys had been protesting that they did not want to stay in the cabin that night, neither did they want Del and Doug to think they were cowards. John closed the door behind them.

It was obvious that nobody had stayed in the building for a long while. The room, which occupied the front half of the crude log building, had a small window at either end. The glass had been knocked out of both, and they were boarded up with rough lumber. The rusted stove was still in place half a yard from the wall and looked as if it hadn't had a fire in it since Scotty's death. Water dripped through several holes in the badly weathered roof.

Del turned to their Inuit friends. "Maybe you were right about finding a better building than this one," he said.

"No." Gust's voice was strong. "We'll stay here. When you go home, we don't want you to tell your friends that we were afraid."

"Besides," John broke in, "I don't believe Scotty comes here looking for his murderer, either."

His Inuit companions stared at him in horror, as though he had spoken some terrible heresy that would get them all struck dead.

"How can you talk that way? You know he threatened to come back and get revenge on the one who killed him. And they say he's been seen up and down the river," Gust reminded him.

"Even the men in our village have seen him!" Stoney said.

While Del and Doug listened intently, Gust recalled the tales they had heard around the fires on long winter nights.

"That's right. He gasped out his threat just before he died! My great-grandfather saw him, and my grandfather saw him. He had a big knife – this long!" He spread his arms wide.

The boys listened to the hammer of rain against the leaking roof and the wind that roared across the mountainous area. It wasn't a pleasant place to be during a storm at night, but they certainly weren't afraid of Scotty's ghost.

Del noisily deposited his gear and headed toward the stove. "I don't know about you guys, but I'm tired of being cold. Let's get a fire going."

John came to help, and together they built a fire in the rusted airtight heater. In a few moments, the flames were roaring pleasantly, and the chill of night was being driven to the far corners of the room.

They sat around the fire quietly. They talked a little, but mostly they listened to the wind. Del wished for an opportunity to talk to them about their need for making a decision to walk with Christ. A few times he tried to get the conversation around to the subject of love and the reason Jesus Christ came into the world, but the Inuit boys' minds seemed to be far away. They scarcely heard what either Del or Doug was saying; and every now and then, a rattling window or the creak of an ill-fitting door would cause them to start.

After a while, Del realized that Gust and John and Stoney actually believed the story of Scotty and his ghostly walks through the old mining camp. His heart ached for them. How terrible it must be to be caught in the grasp of such a superstition.

Finally Doug looked at his watch. "How about going to bed? I'm exhausted."

Gust acted as though he would rather not, but when Del and Doug got into their sleeping bags, he crawled into his too. Stoney and John reluctantly got into theirs too.

The old, abandoned building seemed to be alive. Doors creaked and groaned on their hinges above the mournful sound of the wind, and a loose board banged noisily against the window. In the darkness, every sound was magnified until it was difficult to sleep.

No wonder the Inuit boys were uneasy, Del decided. He couldn't say he blamed them. He didn't feel too good about spending the night in the old house himself. It wasn't that he believed the story they told about old Scotty roaming around the camp looking for his murderer; he knew better than that. But the constant working of the empty building caused him to shiver now and again.

It wasn't long until one of the Inuit boys got up, nervously, and made his way across the creaking floor to the window. Del sat upright. "What's the matter? What's wrong?"

"Oh, nothing." John tried to hide his nervousness. "I got up to see how the storm is doing."

"Scotty isn't roaming around here tonight or any other night," Doug told him. "You don't have to be so scared."

"Who's scared?" the Inuit demanded belligerently. He came back and lay down. "Just because a guy gets up to see if it's still raining is no sign he's scared."

Doug was sorry he had said anything and apologized to John. "I wasn't thinking."

"We should've gone to one of the other buildings," Gust Aposik murmured. "That wouldn't be quite as bad."

"Be quiet and go to sleep," Stoney commanded.

Del turned and glanced quickly in his direction. The darkness was a wall around them, almost isolating them from each other.

For a time the boys were quiet. Del was more asleep than awake when an ear-splitting bang shook the old house. Instantly the boys woke up, jarred to consciousness by the sudden burst of sound.

"W-what was that?" one of the Inuit boys stammered.

For an instant all was hushed.

"What was that?"

"I told you we shouldn't stay here! I told you!" Gust trembled, on the edge of hysteria. "Old Scotty has come!"

An agonized moan escaped John's lips.

"There isn't anything out there," Del said irritably,

getting out of his sleeping bag and fumbling for his flashlight.

The Inuit boys heard him and guessed what he was about to do.

"Don't do it!" Stoney cried. "Don't go out there! Scotty will kill you!"

"Come on, Doug!" Del said. He didn't want to go himself, but something had to be done to quiet their Inuit friends.

"Are you out of your mind?" his brother demanded under his breath. Nevertheless he went along.

The two of them advanced stealthily across the rough board floor, following the wavering beam of the flashlight.

"Do you think there is *someone* out here?" Doug whispered.

"How could there be?"

Del pushed the sagging door open and cried out in surprise.

The Inuit boys jumped to their feet and scrambled for the back door.

"Wait a minute!" Del ordered. "Come back here!"

They stopped reluctantly.

"Come on, I want to show you something."

They hesitated, still afraid to move.

"Come on. I want you to see what scared us so much!"

They did so fearfully, shuffling over the wooden

floor, each one willing to let the others go first. In the doorway they stopped, eyes widening.

"A deer!" they exclaimed in unison. They laughed nervously.

"I guess he must have pushed against the half-open door and broke that old strap that kept it from swinging all the way open," Doug said.

"I thought it was–" Stoney's voice trailed off into the night.

"We were all scared half to death," Doug broke in. "I'm glad it was nothing more than this. I thought it might have been a bear."

"Or worse," Gust added.

They closed the door and went back to their sleeping bags, leaving the startled animal, which was as frightened as they had been.

The night dragged on endlessly. The boys were too wound up to go to sleep. At last, all five managed to doze off.

A new excitement took hold of them as they saw the bright sun and realized that morning had arrived without any harm befalling them. In spite of their weariness, they laughed and joked with one another on the way home.

The first day of the last week of August, the busload of young people from the church in Fairview, Minnesota, left the Alaskan mission and headed home. The Inuit boys got up early and came to tell Doug and Del goodbye. Usually, they were smiling, but on this particular morning their eyes were solemn, and the corners of their mouths drooped.

"We're sure going to miss you guys when we get back home," Doug told them.

"I'll say we are," Del agreed.

John's grin flashed. "It's going to be quiet around here with you gone."

"Yeah," Gust said. "Come back next summer, and we'll have some more good times, okay?"

"Like sinking in quicksand or spending a night at Scotty's old cabin up the river?" Doug knew he shouldn't have mentioned the cabin, but the words slipped out.

Stoney spoke quickly, concern sharpening the thin edge of his voice. "It is better if you don't joke about that."

The others were piling into the bus, when Doug and Del shook hands with their Inuit friends a final time.

"I hope you guys keep on coming here to church every Sunday," Del said.

"We will," Gust assured him.

At that moment, Danny, who was at the wheel of the bus, called out to them. "If you two don't want to be left, get in here."

"We'll be right with you."

They climbed into the bus and took the seats behind the driver and in front of Sandy and her dad.

They all waved good-bye until the mission was out of sight.

"I sort of hate to go home," Doug said. "It's been a great trip."

"I don't think I've ever had so much fun."

"Neither have I. And especially at the gold mine the other night. It was wild."

"Maybe you'd better fill me in," Danny said, leaning back.

"You should've been there, Danny," Del began. "It was so rainy and cold, we decided to sleep in one of the cabins instead of rolling our sleeping bags out on the ground. John and Gust and Stoney were so scared of old Scotty's ghost they couldn't sleep. The wind would rattle a door or a window, and they'd jump ten feet."

"I'm sure it was funny to you guys," Danny said, "but think what it would be like to live in superstition and fear the way they do. And the older they get, the worse it is."

Del was nodding quickly. "It would be weird to spend most of your life being afraid. I'm glad we don't have to be ruled by those things."

Doug was slow in speaking. "If we could have stayed with them for a few more weeks, I believe they would have given their hearts to Jesus."

"So do I. It makes me sorry we have to leave."

"I know how you feel," Danny told them. "Of course, the missionaries are there to bring them the gospel, but associating with Christians every day, the way they were with you, is a lot more effective."

Sandy, who couldn't help hearing what they talked about, pulled in a deep breath. There it was again! She didn't know how many times in the last week or so that she had been reminded how important it was to be with the person you were trying to win for Christ. It was strange, but that thought hadn't even occurred to her until recently. Now she heard it everywhere she went.

Was God trying to tell her something?

Her young body stiffened. Her mother and Robert didn't know Jesus. They wouldn't go to church or allow her even to mention her faith. In one way, it seemed useless to try to break through their stubborn rejection. Still, as long as she was living with them, there was a chance. If she moved out now, they might never become Christians.

Sandy glanced at her dad. That would mean she couldn't move in with him, and she really and truly wanted to. If God might be able to use her more if she stayed with her mother, she couldn't move.

"Dad," she said, tears crowding into her eyes. "I've got something to tell you."

He faced her, staring deeply into her solemn face. "Yes?"

"I hope you'll understand. I really *want* to live with you, but–" As she spoke, a sense of peace and anticipation washed over her. She knew now that

God wanted her to stay with her mother and Robert Fenwick. Sandy still wanted to be with her dad, but that didn't matter anymore. God's will was much more important. And God could somehow make it possible for her to help her dad.

"You don't have to say anymore, honey," he told her gently. "I understand."

"If I stay with Mom, I may be able to lead them to Christ, and that's what we both want, isn't it?"

He gazed out the bus window at the distant hills. "Amen," he said fervently.

* * *

They reached Fairview in less than a week, and about a hundred happy people were at the church parking lot to meet the returning pilgrims. Among the crowd was Dr. Kroeger and his wife. The mission superintendent drew Danny aside and asked, "How did it go? Did you find any prospective missionaries for me?"

"Sure did," Danny answered. "A whole busload."

# THE DANNY ORLIS SERIES

The Danny Orlis series, by Bernard Palmer, delivers a blend of adventure, mystery, and suspense through various settings—from the Canadian wilderness to Guatemalan jungles. Danny Orlis, an adept outdoorsman, skilled athlete, and committed Christian, employs his quick thinking, calm bravery, and biblical solutions to confront everyday problems and hair-raising dangers. Early stories focus on Danny navigating school life, sports, and outdoor challenges, while in later books, Danny and his wife Kay provide wisdom and guidance to youngsters facing lifelike situations and challenges. Having sold over two million copies, this series has made Palmer a renowned author in Christian youth literature. Palmer is also the author of the Felicia Cartright series and various other series for Christian youth.

AVAILABLE FROM WWW.ANEKOPRESS.COM